DOUBLE
VISION
THE
ALIAS MEN

Also by F. T. Bradley

Double Vision

Double Vision: Code Name 711

F.T. BRADLEY

DOUBLE VISION

THE ALIAS MEN

HARPER

An Imprint of HarperCollins*Publishers*

Double Vision: The Alias Men
 For information address HarperCollins Children's Books, a division of HarperCollins Publishers, 195 Broadway, New York, NY 10007.
www.harpercollinschildrens.com

Library of Congress Cataloging-in-Publication Data

Bradley, F. T.

The alias men / by F. T. Bradley. — First edition.

pages cm. — (Double vision ; [3])

Summary: "When Linc Baker heads to Santa Barbara for a family reunion, spy agency Pandora contacts him—again—saying they need his help tracking down a Dangerous Double in Hollywood to prevent worldwide destruction at the hands of a terrorist"— Provided by publisher.

ISBN 978-0-06-210443-4 (hardback)

[1. Spies—Fiction. 2. Impersonation—Fiction. 3. Terrorism—Fiction. 4. Adventure and adventurers—Fiction. 5. Hollywood (Los Angeles, Calif.)—Fiction.] I. Title.

PZ7.B7246Ali 2014 2014001892

[Fic]—dc23 CIP

AC

Typography by Lissi Erwin

14 15 16 17 18 CG/RRDH 10 9 8 7 6 5 4 3 2 1

❖

First Edition

For my parents

PROLOGUE

YOU KNOW IN A MOVIE WHEN THERE'S SOME dude hanging off a cliff or a building, and you stop to wonder how the Hollywood people pulled it off? Because it's all fake. I mean, it's the movies, right?

Only it's not fake. At least not all the time. Like in *The Hollywood Kid*, this movie I was in. There's one part where I was hanging off the—

Anyway, turns out that the scene wasn't fake at all, and there was no stunt double or anything like that. But I should start at the beginning, so you get to hear the whole story.

It all started in my mom's minivan, if you can believe it. But don't worry—like with all Pandora missions, it gets interesting in a hurry. And dangerous, too.

PLACE: HIGHWAY 101, GOING SOUTH

TIME: THURSDAY, 11:25 A.M.

Here's how it all went down.

1

THURSDAY, 11:25 A.M.

"DID YOU REMEMBER TO GRAB GRANDPA'S medicine?" This was Mom talking to my dad, who was driving. We were in the minivan (which kind of smells like french fries and old socks), heading south on California's Highway 101. Our family was about fifteen minutes into the two-hour drive. We were at the part when Mom goes through her mental checklist, making sure we packed up half the house. Next she'd start to worry if she locked the doors and turned the outside lights on.

If you've ever been on a road trip, you know what I'm talking about.

"Grandpa's medicine is in the trunk, with everything else," Dad said. He rolled the window down an inch. "You should really get this thing detailed."

"4BBX329." That was Grandpa talking. He thinks everyone is a criminal, so he keeps track of license plates, since that's how they catch the bad guys on his favorite crime shows. Sometimes Grandpa even writes them down in this little notebook he carries around. And I got to sit next to him in the van while he rattled off letters and numbers, and the occasional vanity plate.

Not that I really cared at that point. I was too busy worrying about a phone call I'd gotten just an hour earlier, when we were still at the house. It was from Albert Black, head of Pandora, this top secret agency tasked with finding dangerous artifacts. I'd been on two missions for them, and I thought that was it for me being a temporary junior secret agent.

See, I'm just a regular kid. The only reason Pandora wants me on these missions is because I look just like a junior secret agent named Ben Green. He's an annoying know-it-all, and—

"Now I'm wondering if I turned the outside lights on," Mom said.

Dad sighed.

Me, I was trying to figure out what job was ahead. On my first mission, to Paris, I was just there to take the place of the junior agent I looked like, Ben Green. On my second mission, in Washington, DC, Pandora had invited me to throw the bad guys off Ben's trail (but I kind of ended up saving the day).

Now Pandora wanted me on a new mission, down in Los Angeles. As it turned out, I was going there anyway. The

Baker family has an annual reunion of sorts every February, where all the aunts and uncles try to impress one another with their cooking and auto-mechanic skills. Mom and Dad even got me out of school for Thursday and Friday, which was a pretty sweet deal. My uncle Tim had this broken-down old car waiting for everyone to fix up, like we did every year. By Sunday the beater would be good as new—an awesome classic car—and we'd have a barbecue to cap the weekend. What can I say: The Bakers know how to turn scrap metal into vintage gold.

"Did you remember to close your bedroom window, Linc?"

"Yes. Also, I locked the back door, and I made sure the auto shop was all secure, too," I said. From my angle, I could see Dad snicker in the rearview mirror. He's an auto mechanic, and his garage, Baker Autos, is conveniently located in our backyard.

"You laugh, but this is important," Mom sputtered when she saw Dad's face.

Now, any other time I would've continued this road-trip razzing of Mom. But right then I was too preoccupied wondering what Albert Black wanted, and what Pandora had in store for me. Black had told me to meet him at two o'clock at the Perfect Frame Café, just up the street from Sterling Studios, a famous movie studio. I was supposed to take a movie-lot tour as part of the mission. Sounds simple enough, right?

But I had that nagging feeling in my gut that I always had

when it came to Pandora missions. Like there was more to it than they were telling me.

At least this time it would be *my* mission, and mine alone. My look-alike, Ben Green, was not invited. So no risk of him messing with my flow. I was kind of excited about that.

"5VAT487," Grandpa mumbled. We were cruising closer to the cliffs along the Pacific now. In the water, tiny-looking surfers were trying to catch a wave, and a coast-guard helicopter hovered in the sky. Grandpa got his nose close to the window. "Geronim*ooooo*," he said.

This was the part where he would start telling us about the time he tried to join the army but they wouldn't let him because of his bad eyesight.

"I was going to be a parachutist, you know," Grandpa said, his eyes still on the sky. "Taking risks, jumping from airplanes and helicopters."

Didn't I tell you? Sometimes when you're family, you already know what the person is going to say before they do. "Sure, Grandpa," I said, like I always did.

"It's true. You know why they yell 'Geronimo' when they jump from the planes?" He didn't wait for us to answer, since we all knew this boring story. "To show they're not scared."

"You seem out of it, Linc," Mom said as she turned in the passenger seat. "Is everything okay?"

"Yeah, sure. Of course it is." I tried a smile. Truth was, I still needed an excuse to get away from the Baker reunion. Even if I only needed to sneak out for an hour or two, when you're twelve, that's not so easy. I'm sure you know what I'm talking about.

She frowned and looked me in the eye with her Mom X-ray vision. I swear, she can see right into my brain. "Something has you worried."

"Well, there is this thing," I said, making things up as I spoke. "Sam's dad knows this guy at Sterling Studios. He offered to give me a free tour." Sam is one of my best friends, and it was the first excuse I could think of.

Mom didn't say anything. I could see Dad glance in the rearview mirror.

"But I don't have to go," I said, feeling the Mom heat. "I mean, it's a really cool opportunity, Sam said." I hoped Mom wouldn't check with his dad on this whopper of a lie I just came up with, or I would be toast. "But I'll just say I can't do it. Because this trip is family time and all," I added.

Mom smiled. "You can go, Linc." She turned back around in her seat.

I exhaled. This lying business was tough stuff. "The tour is at two."

Grandpa glanced over at me. "Movie-studio tour, eh?" He shook his head. "Hollywood, all full of lies and agendas."

And he was right, of course. I just didn't know at the time how right Grandpa was. Not until I got to the mission, anyway.

But it was only an hour tour at Sterling Studios. How bad could it be?

2

THURSDAY, 1:05 P.M.

MY UNCLE TIM AND AUNT JENNY HAVE this really big place in Pasadena—stucco house, pretty flowers, and even a giant backyard with a fire pit. Aunt Jenny is my dad's sister. She restores rusty old cars and sells them for big bucks. Between that and Uncle Tim's real-estate firm, they have a lot more money than us Lompoc Bakers do. Not that I care, but it makes my mom act all weird. Like we have something to prove.

"Oh no." Mom turned to me with this stressed-out, horrified look on her face. "We forgot to bring the wooden ladle." We were unpacking the van.

"It's inside the pitcher." I reached to show her, but then a bunch of cooking supplies fell from the trunk. All over the cobblestone driveway.

Of course that was right when my aunt Jenny came out. She's kind of round and short, and always wears these checkered shirts. "Georgie!" She smiled big and hugged my dad. He rubbed her head, and she pretended to be upset about him messing up her hair. It's like their secret handshake.

Then she moved on to me. "Linc." She smacked my shoulders, like she was trying to squish me. My aunt Jenny has some strength, too, so I rubbed my arms. "Get into trouble lately?" she asked me.

"No," I said, but I could see Dad roll his eyes next to me. "Okay, maybe a little."

Dad coughed.

"Well, those science-lab mice really should be set free," I argued. I was an ambassador of animal rights, if you thought about it.

Aunt Jenny laughed. "That's my boy." Then she gave me a stern look. "As long as you leave your troublemaking in Lompoc. We don't need any mishaps around here."

"Linc will be on his best behavior," Mom said as she walked over. My uncle Tim came outside, still on his cell phone. He's all business when showing houses and talks nonstop, but during these Baker reunions, he kind of hangs back and just watches the car overhaul take place. "Linc!" Uncle Tim called right after he hung up the phone. "What's cookin' with my favorite nephew?"

"I'm your only nephew." We had this same conversation every year. "And there's nothing new, Uncle Tim," I lied, thinking of my Pandora mission.

He hugged me and the rest of the Lompoc Bakers. It's

always awkward with Grandpa. He doesn't like to hug, so there was some grumbling on his part before he went inside the house.

Uncle Tim walked back toward the door, pointing at Dad. "Have Jenny show you the wheels, George. It's a real piece of rust."

"That's how we like 'em," Dad called.

"I have you sleeping in the east-side bedrooms, as always," Aunt Jenny said once Uncle Tim disappeared. Their place is so big, they have whole wings—great for family reunions. Our house in Lompoc is just a little bigger than this wing Aunt Jenny set up for us.

"Thank you." Mom smiled. "Oh, I almost forgot: Linc has some kind of movie-studio tour arranged, at Sterling Studios. Maybe Mike can drive him?"

I froze. "Why can't you or Dad drop me off?" I whispered. Truth was, I didn't want my cousin Mike to tag along on the case.

"Mike will do it. You know how he loves to drive," Aunt Jenny said before I could argue. "That way, your mom and I can talk recipes." She winked at Mom.

"Super," Mom said in her fake excited voice. That was because Mom isn't much of a chef, and Aunt Jenny is.

"Speak of the devil." Aunt Jenny pointed down the tree-lined road, where Mike was driving his white 1960 Ford Falcon. There were a few cars parked along the street—your average sedans, a minivan.

And I spotted one car, a blue compact. There was a woman inside, studying a map but occasionally glancing our way. She had very short silver hair.

Was this lady with Pandora? I didn't recognize her—why was she here?

"Linc!" Dad nudged me.

I looked away from the car. "Huh?"

"Mike's here. Say hello."

Mike had pulled up onto the driveway and rolled down the window. He gave me one of his cool nods. His hair was spiked and looked like he'd used about half a pound of gel to mold it. "Hey." His girlfriend, Willow, had dyed her long hair very blond, and she wore it in two buns on the sides of her head. They looked like earmuffs. She waved hello from the passenger seat.

"Linc needs you to drive him to Sterling Studios for a tour," Aunt Jenny said to Mike, leaning on the car. She checked her watch. "You should probably leave now or you'll hit traffic."

Los Angeles traffic is notoriously miserable, no matter what time of day. But during rush hour it's so bad you might as well walk.

"Sure," Mike said with a shrug. Willow nodded and high-fived Mike from her seat. They're big into high fives, and movies. You can't sit next to them without getting a pop quiz about some random Hollywood flop.

Dad handed me a couple of twenties and told me to behave. Then I got in the back of Mike's car, behind Willow. As I buckled up, I glanced over my shoulder to see if that blue compact was still there.

It was—the woman folded up her map and pulled away.

Mike reversed just in time for me to watch the blue car drive down the street and disappear around the corner. That lady obviously wasn't following me.

I smiled and shook my head. Pandora was turning me into some paranoid agent—like Ben Green.

"What's so funny?" Mike asked.

"Nothing," I said. "Just paranoia."

Mike nodded. "You know what they say about that." He slowly eased to a stop at the end of his street.

"What?" I asked.

Willow answered, "Just because you're paranoid doesn't mean someone isn't out to get you."

"That's what Grandpa always says!" I laughed. It was nonsense; everyone knew that.

Right?

THURSDAY, 1:45 P.M.

I HAD TO GIVE MY COUSIN PROPS, because his shortcuts got us to the Perfect Frame Café fifteen minutes early. Mike spent the whole ride arguing with Willow about some movie they'd seen the night before—Willow thought the ending was too sad, but Mike liked that the main character's best friend died, because it seemed authentic. Me, I tuned out most of the way, thinking of this new mission.

Maybe I'd really ace it this time. That would be cool.

Mike pulled up slowly and lucked into a parking space only half a block down from the Perfect Frame Café.

"I just think he didn't need to die is all," Willow said. She liked to get the last word in.

Mike shrugged and put the car in park. "So Linc, why am

I dropping you here, and not at Sterling Studios?"

"Sam's dad's friend is meeting me here," I lied. I unbuckled my seat belt and grabbed my backpack. Couldn't have Mike asking too many questions. "Mom knows all about it—look, I gotta go."

Mike squinted.

But then he relaxed. "I gotta hustle to meet my friends anyway," he said. "Just need to make sure you're not getting into trouble. Like that time you got stuck in the storm drain."

"I remember." It's a long story for another time. I was eight, and the incident involved a runaway soccer ball, the Pasadena fire and police departments, and me being grounded for a month.

"All right. Call if you need another ride, 'kay?"

I opened my door. "Sure thing." I said good-bye to Mike and Willow and got out.

I watched my cousin pull into traffic, waving his hand out the open window. I tightened my backpack straps, feeling Dad's compass bump against my side. Dad gave it to me before I went to Paris on my first mission, so I'd always know my way home, he said.

I turned to go inside the café but then saw a taxi take Mike's spot, and I heard a familiar voice call from an open window.

"Wait up, kid!" Before the cab had come to a complete stop, Albert Black got out. He's big and round, and today he was wearing a blue shirt and tan shorts. Black quickly paid the driver and watched the cab zip back into traffic before joining me on the sidewalk. "You get here okay?"

"My cousin drove. Don't worry—I told him it was just a studio tour," I added when I caught Black's dark expression. He's an intense kind of guy. I never know if he's going to break into one of his loud laughing fits or if he's going to yell at me for doing something wrong.

Black nodded, and he stopped in his tracks.

"What's wrong?" I asked.

Black turned his face to the sun, closed his eyes, and smiled. "You guys got it good here in California. What's it, seventy degrees out today?"

"Probably. I guess I'm used to it."

"Better than Washington, DC, that's for sure." Black exhaled, and then motioned to the café. "Come on. I'll brief you on the case."

The place was pretty quiet, probably because we were there at two in the afternoon—a little late for lunch, but not dinner, either. Albert Black ordered us some California chicken sandwiches and sodas, and then picked a spot in the back of the café. The surrounding tables were deserted, so nobody could overhear our conversation.

"Your tour of Sterling Studios is at two thirty. We don't have much time," Black said after he ate half his sandwich. The guy has some jaws, because it only took him two bites to get there. He pulled a picture from the breast pocket of his shirt. Slid it across the table. "This is your objective."

I picked up the black-and-white photo. It was a picture of a bowler hat, the kind people wore in the early 1900s. "What's this—some old guy's hat?"

Black glanced around to make sure no one heard. "Not

just anyone's." He leaned across the wobbly café table. "*Charlie Chaplin's* bowler hat."

"It's a Dangerous Double," I said, guessing that it had to be. Dangerous Doubles are these artifacts—identical to real-life ones, only they're very dangerous. Nobody really knows how they get their powers. On my first mission, in Paris, I helped Pandora find a double of the Mona Lisa that hypnotizes people. In Washington, DC, we found the double of George Washington's coat that makes you bulletproof if you wear it. Dangerous Doubles are serious business.

Pandora is this super-secret organization that retrieves these Doubles, to keep us all safe. And now there was a new one to find: Charlie Chaplin's bowler hat.

"That's right—it's a Dangerous Double," Black said, confirming my suspicions. "This hat, if tilted at precisely fifteen degrees . . ." He got close enough for me to spot the stubble of an overdue shave and whispered, "It makes you invisible."

"No way," I said, probably a little too loud.

Albert Black shot me a death-ray stare.

"How do we know this, exactly?"

Black sat back and glanced around the café, and seemed to relax when he saw that the customers still couldn't care less about our conversation. "Honestly? We got lucky, kid. There's a Pandora insider who deals in rare Hollywood antiques. A few days ago, she got a call about an item someone was putting up for sale: a Charlie Chaplin hat that had been stored away in the costume department at Sterling Studios, one rumored within the Pandora intelligence community to have special powers. The guy who'd been running that department for decades, William Redding, was given the hat by Chaplin when Redding was young. Redding passed away, and in his will he gave the hat to his daughter. No one knew he had it until it came up in the will. Not even Pandora."

I tucked the photo of the Chaplin hat in my pocket. "So this daughter has the Dangerous Double?"

Black shook his head. "It's still at Sterling Studios, where Redding kept it. The daughter lives on the East Coast and the antique dealer hasn't picked it up yet—lucky for us, with all the arrangements that had to be made for her father's funeral, she hasn't gotten around to it. But time is running out."

I got what this was about now. "You want me to steal the hat."

Black grinned.

"Why not ask Ben Green to do it? Or is he too squeaky clean for the job, and you need troublemaker Linc?"

Black shook his head.

"Or is this about Pandora not being part of the CIA?" When we were on our mission in Washington, DC, I found some files that said Pandora wasn't a CIA operation. "If I'm going on this mission, you need to tell me the truth."

Black just looked at me. It was kind of creeping me out, but then he said, "You're right: Pandora isn't CIA. *On paper.*" He leaned closer across the table. "Pandora is extreme black ops—that means even members of the CIA don't know we exist. Plausible deniability, Linc."

Black leaned even closer, making the café table dip on his

side. "There's going to be a big reveal at a defense-technology summit in Las Vegas on Monday," he said in a low voice. "It's of a top secret counterterrorism weapon. *Beyond* top secret, actually. A group of defense-contractor engineers invented a drone system—you know what a drone is?"

"An unmanned airplane, right?" I saw it on the news awhile ago. "It drops bombs or does surveillance."

Black nodded. "Only this is a group of drones that can communicate with each other in a highly sophisticated way—don't ask me how; that's the engineers' department. I do know this: When released, these little planes can deliver antidotes to a virus across a city, even across the country."

"Isn't that a good thing?" I asked. "And what does this have to do with the Chaplin hat anyway?"

"Imagine if instead of an antidote, you used the drones to deliver a deadly virus." Black pushed his plate aside. "We've picked up chatter that a terrorist group wants to use it. Their test location is right here."

"Los Angeles?" My throat tightened. I choked on a bread crumb and gulped my soda.

Black nodded. "And from here every major city across the country. This drone system allows the terrorists to maximize impact."

That meant they'd kill as many people as possible. I thought of the Baker clan, tinkering with that rusty car. Mom, making macaroni salad.

I felt sick. I had to save my family. "So you think the terrorists will use the hat to steal that drone-system prototype."

“It’s possible. Bottom line: The Chaplin hat could mean a major security breach at the reveal.” Black leaned close. “Your mission is to get the Dangerous Double.”

“Why me?”

“A big guy like me can’t exactly sneak into a place like Sterling Studios without tipping off security.” He looked me in the eye, and for once Black didn’t look like he was mad at me. “And Ben is on another mission. He can’t get here in time.”

They needed *me*. Linc Baker, the kid with troublemaking skills. Not Ben Green. “Okay, so where am I going, exactly?”

Albert Black nodded and pulled a piece of paper from his breast pocket. When he unfolded it, I saw that it was a map. “Here’s a layout of Sterling Studios. The tour has you sitting on a tram, and will take you from the entrance, here”—he pointed to what looked like a gate shack in front—“around the lot.” He ran his big hand over the paper, following a dotted line.

“Where’s the costume department with the Dangerous Double?”

“Over here, building three hundred.” Black pointed to a large building at the back of the lot. “It’s a warehouse split in two: The front has set props—you’ll have to walk through there to get to the costume department in the back. The front door is the only way in. Oh, and don’t take any of the exits—unless you swipe a staff pass, you’ll set off the alarms.”

“Got it.”

“Now, the tour will just pass by the building, so you’ll

want to break away from the group right around here." He tapped his finger on the dotted line, about a third of the way into the tour. "Jump off the tram. Then you'll sneak inside, grab the hat, and get out."

He made it sound so easy. And it kind of was—I mean, I did sneak into the science lab to set the mice free, right? This was sort of the same thing.

"Redding's will only said the Chaplin hat was in a safe place. No specifics. It might be on a shelf, in a safe, or in a box—so be sure to look everywhere." Albert Black folded the map and slid it my way across the table. "There's security, but they're a bunch of slow surfer types, far as I can tell. You should have at least ten minutes. Oh, and make sure you tell 'em you're fifteen. Otherwise they won't let you on the tour without a parent."

"Okay." I felt butterflies in my stomach. My family's safety was on the line. Suddenly I didn't feel like finishing my sandwich, tasty as it was.

Black dug into his pants pocket, pulled out a cell phone, and handed it to me. "Your new Pandora phone. I'm programmed in there. Call when you secure the Dangerous Double."

I nodded. "Wait—what if I can't find it?"

Black stood up and gave me a dark look. "Then don't bother calling." He leaned on the table. "Secure the artifact, Baker. Whatever it takes."

THURSDAY, 2:20 P.M.

THE STUDIO WAS JUST A BLOCK AWAY, so I walked. Most of LA is not set up for walking—no nice sidewalks, and the whole city is just way too spread out—but here someone had been smart enough to build a path from the studio complex to the strip mall where the café was.

I tightened the straps of my backpack and clutched the compass Dad gave me. It usually made me feel better. But not this time. It only reminded me that my family's lives were on the line.

What if I couldn't find this hat? Much as I hated Ben, he *was* a trained junior secret agent. I was just a regular kid. And Black seemed pretty hard-core about me retrieving the Dangerous Double, with this whole "don't call me unless you find it" business.

I picked up the pace, even though I had plenty of time. But I was surprised to find that there was one of those tourist trams already waiting near the gatehouse at the Sterling Studios entry. A dozen or so people were spread out on the plastic benches, and the tour guide gave me a big thousand-watt smile once I got close. He was a big dude, wearing one of those T-shirts made to show off his biceps. He looked a little orange from too much time on a tanning bed.

"And what's your name, young man?" he asked me, checking his clipboard.

I froze. Was I supposed to be Benjamin Green? On my previous missions, I'd traveled under his name—not cool, since I couldn't stand the guy, but necessary to keep our double status a secret. We'd been able to fool the bad guys more than once.

"Your *name*, little man." The guy looked impatient.

"Linc Baker," I said, going with my gut, wishing Black had told me what to say.

"There you are," the guide said as he checked my name on the board. "Now that wasn't so hard, was it?" More teeth and a fake grin. "How old are you anyway?"

"Fifteen," I lied, just like Black told me.

Tour Guide Guy squinted, and made a big deal of looking me up and down. "Missed a growth spurt or two?" But then he waved to the tram. "You can sit anywhere you like."

I picked the empty bench in the very back, thinking it might give me a quick exit. I was beginning to feel a little nervous as I waited.

What if I got busted? I was very good at causing trouble—at getting away with it, not so much. I was at about fifty-fifty: Half the time I got off, but the other half . . . well, you get the idea. This was going to be a challenge.

"All aboard!" the tour guide called, stirring me from my thoughts. "Choo-choo!"

I realized some lady in a poufy floral dress and lots of curly blond hair was sitting next to me. It would be even harder now to sneak away in the middle of the tour.

The tram jerked, and we slowly made our way through the open gate, past the security checkpoint. The guard waved to us but looked pretty grumpy, like maybe he'd been told to be friendly to the tourists. The lady next to me waved back, but the guard didn't seem to notice or care.

"Welcome to Sterling Studios," the guide told us from his spot next to the driver of the tram. "My name is Greg, and I'll be divulging all of Hollywood's *sss*ecrets to you today." He spoke very close to the microphone, so the speakers overhead made him sound like a hissing snake. "We'll *sss*tart our tour on the west *sss*ide of the lot, and go clockwise until we're back where we *sss*tarted. Oh, and watch out for *ccc*elebrities!" he added with a fake happy tone to his voice. "I hear they're running loose around the studio lot."

Someone laughed at his lame joke. We drove between a warehouse-type building and a small parking lot. There were only four cars there, which made me wonder if this studio was operational at all, or if it was all just fake, like Greg the tour guide.

We drove down a street that looked like a cute little town—the kind of place that sells fudge and antiques. But it wasn't real: You could see the plywood fronts from our angle on the train.

"This is *Sss*terlingville," Greg hissed overhead. "Many movies and TV *ss*series have been *ss*shot here—if you look clo*sss*ely, you might *sss*ee one of the *sss*tars of our hugely popular TV *ss*series *You Only Live Once*."

I'd never heard of the show, but okay.

To the left of me, a fake cameraman was setting up a tripod. He waved. The lady next to me waved back. But I could see the dust on the camera lens as we passed—obviously, this dude wasn't filming anything, except maybe us tourists.

"Hey, Jim," Greg called from in front, waving to the fake camera guy. "To the right, you can see the general store of Sterlingville. This town has been in existence since the studio was first established in 1935." He droned on about all the movies that were shot there, but I tuned the guy out. I had a mission to accomplish.

While the rest of the tourists were hanging out the right side of the tram, I took a minute to pull out my studio map. I followed the dotted line of the tour, past the gate guard and the parking lot, and through this fake little town. Up ahead were more buildings, then we would slowly move eastward to make that clockwise route the guide was talking about. In a few minutes I would have to break away from the tour to get to the costume department building at the far back of the lot.

The lady next to me had her head turned to the general

store, where some couple was pretending to set up for a scene. Greg the tour guide was droning on about this oh-so-popular television series, holding the attention of the rest of the tour. The tram was moving, but very slowly.

Now might be the only chance I had to sneak off.

I inched closer to the edge of my seat. Leaned forward.

I took a step, but then heard the hiss over the tram's intercom behind me.

"Where i*sss* it you think you're going, young man?"

5

THURSDAY, 2:41 P.M.

I FROZE. THEN I RAISED MY HAND, WAV-ing the folded map. "Dropped my paper," I said as I slipped back in my seat. The lady next to me gave me a confused look.

"It appears our young passenger thought he might make a cameo in *You Only Live Once*." Greg the guide fake-laughed at his sad joke, and the group joined him.

I felt my stomach drop as I pretended to laugh, too. I'd just lost my best chance to leave undetected. And we were minutes away from my ideal exit point from the tram.

This was not good.

The tram started moving again, and panic spread through my chest. I had to come up with a plan to get off the tourist tram undetected, or this mission would be a bust.

"Next up, we'll get a glimpse of the departments that make the magic work virtually—our *sss*pecial-effects crew," Greg droned over the intercom. He kept his eyes on me. I needed him to look somewhere else, and for the other tourists to do the same thing.

I needed a distraction.

The tram veered right. I had to hurry up and think of something. An explosion? No dice—I had no way to blow anything up. So what could I do?

"Now, to our left, you can see the restaurant where the stars get their lunch," Greg the guide went on. Having the tourists' attention toward the left side of the tram wasn't good, because that was exactly where I needed to go. I was running out of time!

Then I saw two guys to my right, walking down the street: one short blond dude, one tall guy with black hair. From the back, the tall one kind of looked like this famous actor. And that's when I had my idea. It wouldn't distract the group for long, but then all I needed was a second to slip away.

So I yelled, "Look! It's David Graham!"

Everyone instantly shifted their attention to where I was pointing. The tourists mumbled.

"Everyone, we may have our first *ccc*elebrity *sss*ighting!" Greg hissed.

But I didn't stick around. I slid from my seat, jumped off the moving tram, and ran between the fake restaurant and a pretend barbershop down a dark alleyway toward the back of Sterlingville's Main Street.

I quickly glanced over my shoulder. The tourists were still stretching their necks to catch a glimpse of David Graham, who totally wasn't there.

Behind the fake storefronts was a wide street. A few golf carts were parked in front of a large warehouse-type building across the street to my left—298 was written in big black letters near the door. A group of people carrying clipboards huddled nearby, but thankfully, they didn't pay attention to me.

To the right, there was another building—299. And I caught a glimpse of a large warehouse to the right of it. That had to be the costume department!

I passed a woman on the phone, and a guy driving a golf cart who gave me a smile and a nod. There was a girl with long dark hair, carrying a big bag, walking in the opposite direction—she looked familiar, and I figured she was an actress or something. Nobody seemed to pay much attention to me, which was a good thing.

I reached the building—300. My hand almost slipped off the door handle, my palm was so sweaty. I reminded myself that this was a simple mission.

Get the hat. Get out. Save my family—and the rest of LA—from evil terrorists. Easy-peasy, right?

Inside, the warehouse smelled a little like old books at a library. There was a front waiting-type area with chairs lining the walls, and a small reception desk. Thankfully, no one seemed to be working.

I slipped behind the desk and into the warehouse. The

place was full of shelves that reached the ceiling—it reminded me of this auto-parts place up in Pismo Beach where Dad goes to get supplies. Only here the shelves were filled with furniture from different eras. I passed chairs, tables, and lamps from the fifties, the seventies—even stuff that looked like it belonged in a Western movie.

But where was the hat? Was there a safe someplace?

I turned and went down another aisle. More furniture, and clear plastic containers marked *Bedding, '70s* and *Accessories, Girl's Bedroom*, and *Rolled-up Rugs*. I stopped, feeling hopeless. How was I supposed to find a hat in this giant building?

I had to get to the back half of the warehouse, Black had told me. To the costume department. Then I caught a glimpse of a door at the end of the aisle I was in. *Costumes*, it said in curly black letters. Eureka!

I rushed toward the back of the building. There were windows on either side of the door, but it looked dark behind them. I tried the door. It was open—I couldn't believe my luck. This mission might just be a piece of cake after all.

I found the light switch to the left as I walked inside. Waited for the flicker of the overhead lights. And then my good mood faded with the darkness. This space was as big as the front half of the warehouse behind me, only it was lined with double-high racks of clothing, interspersed with shelves.

I groaned. Why couldn't this just be easy?

But there was no time to whine about it. I had to get to work, before Tour Guide Greg realized I was missing.

I combed the rows of musty-smelling dresses, suits, and coats. There were clear plastic containers with shoes inside, stacked high on the shelves down one of the aisles. I didn't see a safe, so I wondered if maybe the Dangerous Double was hidden in plain sight.

"Hats, I need hats," I mumbled. These Pandora missions were so stressful, I was turning into Grandpa, talking to myself.

Finally, I found an area with big round hatboxes—this had to be it, right? But which one had the Chaplin hat, my Dangerous Double? Thankfully, each box was neatly labeled: *Ladies, 1930s* and so on. What was Chaplin's hat again? I pulled the picture Black had given me from my pocket, and took a quick glance. Right—a bowler hat. That was what I needed.

I was about halfway down the aisle with the hatboxes when I heard the faint sound of a door opening then closing at the other end of the warehouse, where I'd come in.

I froze.

"Hey, kid!"

THURSDAY, 2:51 P.M.

"HEY!" GREG THE GUIDE HOLLERED AGAIN from the prop area. "You're gonna get me fired. Nobody's allowed to just run around the lot. Come out—I know you're in here!"

I wasn't giving up now. Not when I was so close. So I hurried down the aisle, frantically looking for the bowler hat.

And there it was! It even said on the little label: *Chaplin Bowler*. I couldn't believe my luck when I opened the box and pulled out the hat.

"I'll find you, you little pain in the rear," Greg said, sounding much closer now.

I quickly stuffed the bowler hat inside my backpack. Then I hurried toward the door I'd come in through, and turned off the light.

"Ah—looking for costumes, are you?" I heard Greg's footsteps nearby. He must have seen the lights go off through the windows by the door.

I should've just left the lights on. Now he had me.

I saw the door handle inch down. I slipped between some poufy Mary Poppins dresses, hoping Greg wouldn't find me.

"You know, you might as well come out," Greg called as he came in through the door to the costume department. "I already called security." He closed the door behind him.

I held my breath. These dresses could've used some dry cleaning, let me tell you.

"Sterling Studios doesn't tolerate trespassing, you know." Greg sounded very close now. "You'll go to kid prison, sport." He stood right next to me. I could see his white shoes under the dresses. And he saw me, too. "Ha!" he yelled, and reached into the rack of dresses.

But this wasn't my first getaway, in case you're wondering. So I darted deeper into the rack of dresses and then slipped out. Except one of those skirt hoops got stuck on the zipper of my backpack. And before I knew it, I saw the whole rack come down.

Right on top of Greg the guide's head. He struggled, and looked like he was being attacked by all those dresses.

I laughed. It was funny, right?

Then I saw two security guards opening the door to the costume department. And Albert Black was wrong—they weren't surfer dudes. Sure, they were tanned, but they also looked pretty serious about their jobs.

So I quickly turned around, and stared right at Greg. He had a hoop skirt stuck on his head, making him look ridiculous.

But I didn't laugh this time. Because the two guards approached behind me, and I knew there was no way out of this jam.

I was busted.

7

THURSDAY, 3:00 P.M.

THE GUARDS TOOK ME AWAY, RIGHT after they helped Greg wrangle that hoop skirt.

"Make sure this kid never makes it back onto Sterling Studios property," Greg huffed on his way out to meet the stranded tourists. "Blacklist him!"

The guards had gotten there on bicycles, but they ended up walking alongside the bikes as we made our way to the small office building near the warehouse.

"What on earth were you doing over there, kid?" the older of the guards asked me. He looked friendly enough.

I shrugged. "Just curious, I guess." I glanced at the guy's partner, a tall skinny dude with thin reddish hair. He was carrying my backpack with the Dangerous Double inside. I didn't really care what happened next, as long as I could complete this mission.

"You know, we'll have to call the authorities now," the older guard said. We passed a group of guys, one with a folder, all of them giving us a sideways glance.

"The police?" I said.

I was thinking about calling Albert Black to bail me out, when this skinny guy walked up to us. His hair was bleached blond, he wore brown plastic glasses, and under a leather jacket I saw a Rolling Stones T-shirt. He walked kind of bouncily on bright orange sneakers.

Whoever he was, this odd-looking dude made the guards stop in their tracks. "Mr. Floyd," the older guard said.

Floyd pointed at me. "Who's the kid?"

"Lincoln Baker," I said. Mr. Floyd was obviously important, or otherwise no one would have let him get away with wearing that getup, so I straightened. "Everybody just calls me Linc."

"You're brilliant, Linc," Floyd said with a big smile. He had a British accent.

The older guard cleared his throat. "Actually, Lincoln Baker here broke into the costume department warehouse. We're detaining him until the police arrive."

Floyd nodded, like he was agreeing with the older guard. I guess I wasn't so brilliant after all. But then Floyd shook his head and said, "Forget about all that. Let the kid go."

I smiled. "Yeah. That's a great idea."

Floyd studied my face. "For the last two days, I've been

watching every bloomin' child in this city audition for my film. They're all awful. But you . . ." He grabbed my chin and moved my face. Studied my profile from each side. "You're just the kid I'm looking for."

"You're casting him in your movie?" the tall guard asked.

Uh-oh. "I'm not an actor," I said. "So you've got the wrong guy."

Floyd shook his head. Pulled a pen and piece of paper from the inside pocket of his jacket. "It's settled. Come to this address—my humble abode," he said with a smile as he handed the paper over. "Seven o'clock. We're having a little bash to celebrate a friend's Oscar nomination, yeah?"

If it got me out of this jam with Sterling Studios security, why not, right? "Um, okay."

"You're perfect for the role." Floyd tucked the paper in my palm. "Be there tonight and I'll make sure my assistant, Larry, gets you the contract for your agent, Lincoln—what was it again?"

"Baker."

"*Lincoln Baker.*" He smiled. "Marvelous." He turned and waved his hand over his shoulder as he walked away. "Absolutely marvelous!"

The guards looked kind of lost, there on the studio sidewalk. I glanced at the piece of paper in my palm. Stuffed it in my pocket.

"Well, buddy," the old guard said with a sigh, "I guess you're a movie star."

I was about to object to this, when the tall guard handed me my backpack. "Good luck."

"So I can leave now?" I asked.

The guards nodded.

I smiled. I found the Dangerous Double—and got busted—but still managed to walk out with the hat. I saved my family, all in like an hour. It couldn't have ended better than this.

Albert Black would be thrilled, and now I could go back to my aunt and uncle's place to spend the weekend with the Baker clan.

Perfect ending to a perfect day, I thought as I walked past the security shack and back to the café. Albert Black was waiting for me at the curb, about to light one of his stinky cigars.

"Back already, kid?" Black tucked the cigar in the breast pocket of his shirt. "They kick you out?"

I shook my head, and couldn't help grinning. "I got the hat!"

"Shhh!" Black glanced around, but there was only some woman with a stroller trying to get inside the café, too busy to notice us. He relaxed. "Let's see it."

I got closer. Unzipped the large compartment of my backpack. And reached inside to pull out the bowler hat. "Do we need to be careful?" I asked Black. "You know, so we don't go invisible in the middle of LA?"

Albert Black groaned. "You're gonna wish you were invisible." He pulled the hat from my backpack and shoved it in my face. "Read the label on the inside."

Made in China.

"So what?"

"This is a cheap knockoff Chaplin hat—made in the past decade, at best."

I felt my heart stop. "This isn't the Dangerous Double."

Albert Black shook his head. "You got the wrong hat, kid."

"But there wasn't another one. And it said 'Chaplin Bowler' on the box," I added.

"It was there when the costume department head died." Black's face went dark. "Maybe someone beat you to it."

My heart skipped a beat. "Did that terrorist group get the Dangerous Double?"

Black shook his head. "They're not in the US—not yet anyway."

"Some safe place, this warehouse," I mumbled.

Black said, "Word is, William Redding practically lived at that costume department, never even took a sick day. He guarded the Chaplin Dangerous Double. The costume department was a very safe place to keep it. Until he died, that is."

"So do I have to go back to Sterling Studios? This dude Greg really hates me, and there's some strange director guy in orange sneakers who wants me to be in his movie."

Black pulled my arm. "Wait—what director?"

"I don't know." I pulled away. "He said I was perfect for his movie or something. He had a British accent—Floyd," I added, remembering the guy's name now. "Weird dude."

"Nigel Floyd—he's a famous movie director, kid." Black

smiled. "This might just work out after all. It's possible someone on that Sterling Studios movie lot took the Dangerous Double before we could get to it. Security around here is obviously tight enough that it has to be a staff member. This person probably doesn't even know about the powers of the Chaplin hat."

"So now what?" I stuffed the stupid bowler hat inside my backpack and zipped it up.

"Floyd loves you." Black smacked my shoulder. "This is a perfect way in. We can find out if someone took the Dangerous Double. Steal it back."

I felt a familiar feeling in my gut, the kind I'd had on my previous missions. Like Pandora just dropped a brick inside my stomach. "I have to go to this party tonight? I'm no actor," I muttered.

"You are now." Black grinned. "Welcome to Hollywood, kid."

THURSDAY, 3:30 P.M.

I CALLED MY COUSIN, AND HE PICKED ME up outside the Perfect Frame Café. During the drive back, Mike and Willow argued about the right amount of butter on popcorn (Willow said none was best, while Mike thought popcorn should be drenched in it). All I could think about was these bad terrorist dudes. The Dangerous Double. The drone weapon that could kill everyone in Los Angeles.

The thought of buttered popcorn made me feel sick to my stomach.

As we got closer to Pasadena, I tried to come up with a cover story to tell my parents. How was I going to talk them into letting me go to some famous director's house that evening? Twelve-year-olds don't go to fancy Hollywood parties.

As we walked up to my aunt and uncle's place, I still didn't know what to do. But thankfully, my dad and my aunt Jenny had their heads buried under the hood of a rusty car that was parked inside the garage. There were car parts strewn all over the lawn—a bench seat, a rusty battery, even the steering wheel wasn't where it should be.

"Dude, this is a disaster," I whispered to Mike.

Mike just shrugged. Willow made a face and disappeared inside.

"Linc!" Dad got out from under the hood of the car and smiled. His face was smeared with oil, and his glasses had slid to the tip of his nose. "Isn't she a beauty?"

"She's something."

Aunt Jenny came over and wiped motor oil on my cheek. "In a few days, this will be a mint 1940 Cadillac Town Car—just you watch."

"You gotta see the potential, Linc." Dad put his hand on the rust-colored metal. "She doesn't know it herself, but we'll show her." He always talked about cars like they were people. "Come on inside. We'll go see Mom."

Mom looked up from her cutting board when we made it to the kitchen. The place looked like the vegetables had been in battle, and they were all casualties. "How was the tour?" she asked.

I hesitated, and then decided my best bet was not something I would ordinarily do. Any other situation, I'd come up with a good story, something that Mom and Dad would buy. But instead I rolled the dice.

I told them the truth.

"Wait—you're cast in a movie?" Mom stopped cutting celery. "By a famous director, no less."

"Nigel Floyd or something," I said, adding a shrug.

Mom frowned. "It sounds like one of your made-up stories."

"It's the truth!" I argued.

Dad jumped in, thank goodness. "Seems like a cool opportunity, Linc."

"So can I go?" I asked. "To this party tonight?"

"Isn't there paperwork to sign?" Mom frowned. "I should really talk to the director."

"No need," I said quickly. "I can just bring the paperwork home. Floyd said he'll have it at the party."

Mom pointed the knife at me. "You can't miss the reunion picnic. I don't care what the shooting schedule is. I'll have to see this contract. Oh, and you'll have to let me know where you are *at all times*."

"Sure, yeah." I felt relief push away that brick in my stomach. "Can you put the knife down, Mom?"

She looked at her hand, and then shook her head with a smile as she placed the knife on the cutting board. "I'm so . . . frazzled." Mom sighed. "These picnics always turn into such a stressed weekend. I just hope my pasta salad tastes okay."

Mom's pasta salad stinks, if you want to know the truth. But don't tell her that. The only dish she can pull off is spaghetti and meatballs, and I'm pretty sure the meatballs come frozen and the sauce is from a jar. "You'll be fine," I lied. "So can I go to this party?"

"As long as Mike agrees to join you, we have a deal."

Thankfully, Mike never got the memo about having to come with me to the party. I mean, joining me could mean just driving, right? So technically I wasn't lying.

"Sure, cuz," he said when I asked him for a ride. "I'm heading to Santa Monica to hang on the pier with my guys. I can drop you off before."

After dinner, we took off from the house at six thirty and hit the highway. Willow wasn't coming along this time, and Mike was pretty quiet until we took the exit to the 110.

"So you're gonna be in a movie, huh?" He smiled and nodded. "That's super cool, man."

"Yeah." Truth was, the idea of being on camera scared me more than being chased by bad dudes on a Pandora case.

"Hey, think you can get me a spot?" Mike gave me his cockiest of grins.

"I'll try."

"That would be cool, right?" He nodded to himself. "Be in a real Nigel Floyd movie. *Man.*" He smiled.

If I could, I'd give him my spot.

We didn't talk the rest of the way, and Mike turned the radio to some heavy metal. Not that I was listening. As we passed Culver City (no traffic, which was a miracle) and exited the 110 at the Pacific Coast Highway along the beach, I couldn't stop thinking about the Dangerous Double.

Who had it? What if this bad-dude terrorist group got

ahold of it and used it to get into the conference and take the drone weapon?

"Hey, Linc." Mike pushed my shoulder. "We're here, man."

I looked up and realized we'd already arrived in Malibu and were driving up a winding road. Mike stopped a dozen yards from the double metal gates.

"Can't go farther," Mike said, pointing at the gates. "Unless you take me with you." He gave me a hopeful glance.

I shook my head. "No, invitation only. Sorry," I added, hoping I sounded like I meant it. I couldn't risk Mike getting caught in the middle of the Pandora mission.

Mike shrugged. "Call me if you need a ride back."

I got out and felt the cool breeze coming from the Pacific. It was getting dark, but I could still see the water below. This had to be the best place to live in California. I pulled the straps on my backpack tighter, feeling the compass swing on the clip, reminding me why I was here.

I watched Mike's taillights disappear, and geared up to go to this party. I took a deep breath and tried to clear my head to focus on the mission. Get the Dangerous Double.

But then I saw a white van pull up and stop on the side of the road. The driver flashed the headlights—just once, but it was enough for me to know: Albert Black was here.

When the cargo side door slid open, I was greeted by a face I hate more than anyone's in the world.

Benjamin Green.

THURSDAY, 7:00 P.M.

THE WORST THING ABOUT BEN GREEN? HE looks almost exactly like me. Take away the cocky grin and the standard-issue black cargo pants and we might as well be twins. Only he's a by-the-book, know-it-all junior secret agent, and I'm the exact opposite. Needless to say, I can't stand the guy.

"Get in, Baker," he said.

Since there was a red sports car waiting to pass the van, I did. It wasn't until I got inside that I took a good look at Ben's outfit. He was wearing a pair of blue swimming trunks and a green shirt with I Love LA on it.

I laughed. "Dude, did a tourist shop throw up on you?"

Ben shot me a death-ray stare. "The airline lost my

luggage, so I had to buy provisions at the airport."

"The outfit is totally working for you," I said, still laughing. His pale legs looked lost without long pants to protect them, and his toes wiggled in oversized flip-flops. I would bet my video-game collection that Ben had never worn anything but secret agent boots in his life.

"Enough with the joking," Albert Black called from the passenger seat.

I saw Agent Stark, his secret agent sidekick, in the driver's seat. She looked serious as ever, in a black turtleneck, her brown hair pulled back in the usual bun. "Hey, Agent Stark."

"Linc," she said with a nod.

"So why the welcoming committee?" I asked, but I had a sneaking suspicion. Ben Green was here for a reason, and it wasn't to get a California gift-shop wardrobe.

"Since the mission has become more"—Albert Black searched for words—"of a pain in the you-know-what, we pulled Agent Green off another mission and flew him in."

"You're replacing me," I said.

Everyone in the van was silent.

"And you think fake surfer boy here is going to do a better job finding the Dangerous Double than me?" I had to clench my fists to keep from blowing up. This was *my* case, *my* turf, *my* family's lives on the line.

"I'm a trained agent," Ben said, crossing his arms. "If it had been me on the Sterling Studios tour, the artifact would be secure by now."

"No it wouldn't," I argued. "The Dangerous Double was

already gone when I got there."

"At least I wouldn't have been detained by security," Ben countered. "Or brought back a made-in-China imitation piece."

"There was no way I could've had time to—"

"Silence!" Black yelled from his seat in front. "The point is, I can't risk any more mistakes. The unveiling of the drone system is on Monday at nine a.m., and here we are, Thursday night, back at square one." He looked at me. "Green is going in, and you're going home, Baker. It's decided."

"But I'm the one who got cast in the movie!"

"And now Agent Green will take your place."

I looked to Agent Stark, but it was obvious she wasn't going to have my back this time. I was out. Ben Green was in. I reached for the van door handle.

"Stay here, Baker," Black barked. "I'll call a cab. Don't want you getting any ideas, like sneaking off to this party."

I shrugged, like it was no big deal that I got replaced by my annoying double. But secretly, I wanted to know about the mission.

"Now, Agent Green," Stark said to Ben. "We think we know who stole the Dangerous Double from the warehouse." She handed him a photograph, but I snatched it away before Ben could take it.

"Let me see it," I said. First they have me do all the work, and then I'm supposed to just let Ben Green take over? I don't think so. I caught a quick glimpse of the photograph. It was a gritty image, like maybe it came from some security camera.

The picture was of an average-height guy, kind of skinny, with dark hair, a mustache, and a cream-colored suit. He looked rich.

"Gimme that." Ben pulled the photograph from my hand.

"Who's the dude?" I asked.

Stark hesitated, but then said, "His name is Ethan Melais. He's a professional con man—a thief of secrets. He sells them to whoever is willing to pay top dollar." She kept her eyes on Ben. "A freelance spy."

Albert Black dialed a number on his phone. From his hushed conversation, I could just make out that he was calling a cab.

"How does Melais get these secrets?" I asked.

"This isn't your case, Baker," Ben said. But then he looked at Stark, waiting for her to answer my question.

"Ethan Melais has a knack for getting himself into closed-door meetings—he's just that good a con man. We had a Pandora meeting here in Los Angeles yesterday." Stark clenched her jaw. "We have reason to believe he got in, found out about the Chaplin hat."

Ben groaned.

Stark continued, "Intelligence tells us he's planning to infiltrate the top secret conference on Monday, so he can sell the drone-system prototype to the terrorist group."

"The world would be like an all-you-can-eat buffet of secrets if this Melais guy got the hat," I said. "He wouldn't have to con his way into anyplace. He could walk right in, and no one would be the wiser."

“And this is the only image we have of our suspect?” Ben waved the gritty photograph. “Assuming the hair and clothing could be changed—”

“That’s useless,” I mumbled. It was true: I wouldn’t recognize Melais if he was sitting right next to me in this stuffy van.

“It’s what you have,” Stark snapped. “Linc: You just sit here and wait for that cab,” she said to me before pulling herself together. “Green: Get to work. Find Ethan Melais. Bring us the Dangerous Double.”

Ben asked, “Do you think he’s here?”

Stark nodded. “The Chaplin hat gave us a lucky break in the hunt for Ethan Melais. There have been confirmed cases of top-secret-information theft in Rome, Moscow, and Frankfurt. It turns out that Nigel Floyd had a production in these locations at the same time as the thefts.”

I said, “Ethan Melais is a movie guy. He’s part of Floyd’s crew.”

“That’s still a very broad category,” Ben commented. He was right, but I wasn’t going to admit that.

“Before, we didn’t have much of anything,” Stark said, “so this is a breakthrough in the case. We may have come here to retrieve the Dangerous Double and secure the drone-system prototype, but now our objective has expanded.”

“Find Ethan Melais, find the Dangerous Double,” I said, summing up the case.

“Exactly.” Stark pointed up the drive, to the gates to Nigel Floyd’s mansion. “That party is the best place to start. Ethan

Melais is part of the movie crew. He's simply waiting until Monday, when he can steal the drone-system prototype and make a fortune."

"So our perp profile is that Melais is male, average height, and slender. I'll go inside," Ben said with one of his annoying super-serious nods.

"And you're going home, Baker," Black said. He'd ended his phone call and had been listening to our conversation. "A cab will be here in five minutes."

Ben Green pushed past me and opened the sliding door to get out of the van. Before he jogged up to the gate, he glanced over his shoulder and smiled.

I won, Baker.

And I had no choice but to let him hijack my mission.

The cab must've been nearby when Black called, because it pulled up right as Ben made his way past the gate. This was just great, I thought, as Black gave the guy a wad of cash to drive me back to Pasadena. Ben was going to get Ethan Melais and the hat, even though I had the most to lose.

No way.

Black got back into the van, and as I opened the passenger door of the cab, this flashy Mercedes SUV that I knew cost more than a hundred thousand bucks drove by.

Then the driver slammed the brakes. Backed up.

The tinted window rolled down, and a guy with bleached-blond hair leaned across the passenger seat. "Lincoln Baker, my man. You made it!" Floyd had a big smile on his face.

"Yeah, but . . ." I pointed at the cab. "I have to go."

"Nonsense!" Floyd said, and he popped the passenger door. "Get in."

I glanced over my shoulder at the van. This was my chance to save my family, plus stick it to Pandora for ditching me. I'd catch Ethan Melais, get the Dangerous Double. Save everyone from the bad guys and their evil plans.

"Okay." I waved the cabbie off and got into the Mercedes SUV.

Floyd hit the gas before I even put my seat belt on. "I hope you're ready to party, Linc."

10

THURSDAY, 7:28 P.M.

LOS ANGELES IS AN EXPENSIVE PLACE TO live. And judging from Floyd's house, I was pretty sure he had the most expensive place in the city. From the gate and past some trees I caught glimpses of a concrete mansion with tall windows and an enormous balcony. No doubt it had a killer view of the Pacific.

"Can you believe I'm late to my own party?" Floyd said with a laugh. "Stupid bean counters and their meetings—all they worry about is money."

I had no idea what that was about, so I just nodded.

Beyond the metal gates, we passed dense bushes and aloe plants. Then we came to a circular driveway with a tiered fountain in the middle. Floyd zoomed past a line of cars and cut in front.

We got out. He tossed the keys to one of the valets. "Put it in the garage, next to the Aston Martin, yeah? Scratch it up and you're dead, bloke," he said to the guy.

The valet laughed, but you could tell he wasn't sure if it was a joke. Come to think of it, neither was I.

"Come on, Linc," Floyd said as we walked up the wide steps of his mansion. The place was enormous, and everything was straight-lined and metal—like those fifties houses, only brand-new and mansion-sized. There were double wooden doors that a butler-looking guy opened for us. For someone like me who was used to doing that myself, it was kind of awkward.

And the butler was wearing a Chaplin hat! As soon as we made it inside, I saw several butlers with the same getup: white shirt, bowler hat—all that was missing was a mustache.

"What's with the Chaplin hats?" I asked Floyd.

"Part of the ambience, Linc." He spread his arms, obviously proud of his house and the big party he was throwing. "We're celebrating the origin of the Academy Awards, going all the way back to the first Oscars, in 1929. Honoring the masters, like Chaplin, yeah?"

"Yeah. I mean, sure." This was going to make my job even harder. Any one of those hats could be the Dangerous Double. All Ethan Melais had to do was tilt the hat and he'd disappear. Reminded of the mission, I wondered where Ben was. Had he made it inside?

What if Floyd caught us together? My whole kid-actor cover would be a bust.

This could get complicated. I had to hurry and find that

Ethan Melais dude, so Pandora would send Ben on his way and victory could be mine. I tried to think of a way to lose my annoying look-alike, but then Floyd pulled me by the arm.

"This way." We left the marble-tiled entry and walked into a giant space that looked like his living room. There were white sofas, a red coffee table, and a black grand piano. The back wall was made out of sliding doors that opened up to a huge deck, showing a view of the sun setting over the Pacific in the distance.

"Whoa," I whispered, looking around the place, forgetting I was supposed to be cool.

Floyd laughed. "You like it? I don't know, I was thinking it's a little predictable, you know? So Hollywood." He motioned to the glass wall. "Come on, let's go on the deck."

We walked outside, passing groups of party guests who nodded to Floyd or shook his hand in passing. This dude was a big shot. To be honest, I was feeling a bit nervous. Bakers aren't exactly a fancy bunch.

I scanned the crowd for Ethan Melais suspects: an average height, skinny male. But it was pointless. Dozens of dudes at this party could be him, let's face it. It seemed so easy: Find one bad guy with a Chaplin hat. But like every Pandora mission, it got more complicated in a hurry.

Below the deck, there was this awesome pool surrounded by lounge chairs. Down the grassy hill from the mansion stood a small ranch-style house.

"That's the old place," Floyd said when he caught my eye. He leaned on the deck railing. "It's where I got my humble beginning, before all this." He motioned to the mansion, the deck, the pool, the perfectly manicured lawn. "I still go down there sometimes, when I need to think."

"Looks a lot like my house," I said.

Floyd looked a little sad. "I miss the days when it was all so simple."

"Who is your new friend, Nigel?" A woman in black pants and a big white blouse came up from behind Floyd. She had shoulder-length blond hair and wore pink-framed glasses. I guessed she was about my mom's age. She extended her right hand, and leaned on Floyd's shoulder with her left. "I'm Katherine Freeman. You can call me Kate. I'm the makeup artist."

Floyd said, "Kate here is nominated for an Academy Award. She's the guest of honor for this little soiree."

"Wow," I said.

"I think the guests are actually here for you," Kate said to Floyd. "But it's a nice party."

"We go way back—Kate and I were roommates once, living just down that hill, isn't that right?"

Kate nodded. "I still remember coming to the city with nothing but my suitcase. If Nigel hadn't taken me in as a roommate, who knows where I'd be?"

"And then my friend Larry moved in," Floyd added with a grin. "The three musketeers, we called ourselves. Like Charlie Chaplin, Douglas Fairbanks, and Mary Pickford—they were friends in their early Hollywood days and eventually started their own film company, United Artists, you know."

"Is that what you're going to do—start your own company?" I asked.

Floyd smiled. "In my dreams. But so far we've done almost every movie together, right, Kate? Except for this last one you got the Oscar nod for."

"We make a good team," she said.

"But you live in this mansion now," I said to Floyd.

Floyd nodded. "The place down there is empty. We've all moved on, haven't we?"

Kate nodded, looking a little sad. She turned her attention to me. "We haven't even been introduced. You must be Nigel's new protégé."

"I'm Linc Baker," I said.

Floyd said, "He's a star. Completely genuine—just the fresh innocence we need." Floyd's phone rang. When he saw the caller ID, he frowned. "Gotta take this, but you enjoy the food, okay? There's a video-game room on the lower floor."

And before I could say anything, Floyd disappeared in the crowd of party guests.

Kate gave me a smile. "He's a little . . . intense."

"No kidding." The wind blowing up the hill was getting colder now, and the sunset had given way to dark skies.

Kate pointed to the living room. "Come on. Let's get inside and eat."

I followed her, and we settled somewhere near a bar. I looked around for Ben, but I still didn't spot him in the crowd. I wondered if he'd found Ethan Melais yet. I wanted to be the one to bring Melais in.

Kate ordered us both sodas. After handing me mine, she studied me with X-ray eyes, like Mom's. "So you're the muse?"

"The what?"

She laughed. "Floyd's muse—do you know anything about movies, Linc?"

I shook my head. No point in lying, I figured. "I don't even know what this movie is about."

Kate said, "*The Hollywood Kid* is a creative interpretation of the silent-film classics as juxtaposed against today."

Huh?

When she saw my confused look, Kate laughed and added, "The film is a collection of modern vignettes, seen through the eyes of a child of the 1930s." She pointed at me. "Through *your* eyes."

"I'm this Hollywood kid or whatever?"

She nodded.

"No pressure or anything," I mumbled.

Kate smiled. "Have you seen Charlie Chaplin's *The Kid*?"

I shook my head.

"That's what Nigel's film is based on—creatively, anyway. *The Kid* is thought to be based on Chaplin's poor childhood in the UK."

I nodded and pretended to pay attention. But really, I was scanning the crowd for skinny dudes who could be Melais. There were lots of them, unfortunately.

"The Tramp is really a genius character," Kate went on. "Did you know he came up with the costume himself? Chaplin just gathered clothing from fellow comedians. He added the mustache so he'd look older."

"That's where he got the bowler hat?"

Kate nodded. "There were many other bowler hats over the years, of course." She smiled. "Anyway, we should eat before it's gone." She motioned to the buffet up ahead. Instead of having legs, the three tables were suspended from the two-story ceiling by heavy chains.

From afar I could see there were a bunch of little appetizer snacks—my favorite. But I wasn't here to eat. I had to find Ethan Melais, tonight. Before he could get the drone-system prototype and sell it to the terrorists. "Maybe later," I said.

"Don't wait too long," Kate said. "Hollywood is like any other place. People will take what they can get before someone else does." And she was off to get her plate.

I looked around, taking in my surroundings. There were lots of people, some looking dressy in suits, some wearing jeans and ratty T-shirts, like they were too cool to make an effort. And lots of skinny dudes, unfortunately.

I glanced up to the second-floor balcony, which overlooked the great room. And that's when I spotted someone. A familiar-looking girl with long black hair, wearing jeans and a white blouse. She turned around and waved.

To me?

I looked over my shoulder to make sure there wasn't some handsome kid behind me—nope, just me. So I went upstairs, passing some people dancing to the jazzy music that was playing from the speakers.

I walked over to the pretty girl, hoping my smile wasn't too dorky. Trying to be cool, even though I was pretty sure I was working on some sweaty pit stains.

"I'm Savannah." She shook my hand. I remembered now: I'd seen her at Sterling Studios, when I was looking for the warehouse. Her handshake was firm. "You're the other kid."

"Huh?" Was she talking about Ben? I glanced around, but he wasn't in sight.

Savannah frowned, but only with her left eyebrow, which for some reason made her even prettier. "The other kid in Floyd's movie. I'm the girl lead."

"Oh," I said, sighing in relief. "*The Hollywood Kid*. Yeah, that's me. Linc Baker."

Savannah leaned closer. She smelled like fresh laundry. "Did Nigel put you through the wringer too when you auditioned? I had to come back three times."

"Not me. We just met on the Sterling Studio lot when I was taking a tour, and Floyd talked me into the job."

Savannah made a face like she just ate a sour piece of candy. "You're kidding. Have you ever even been in front of a camera?"

"Only when Mom pulls out the home recorder for my birthday," I joked, and realized I should've kept my mouth shut.

Savannah was practically exploding. She took a step back, but ended up against the balcony railing. "You're an amateur. Do you even know how hard the rest of us have to work to— never mind." She pushed past me.

"Wait," I mumbled, but I knew it was useless. I'd messed up, and it wasn't even my fault. How could I help it that Floyd picked me?

I turned and looked over the balcony, hoping to see Melais down below. And that's when he looked up: Benjamin Green. Looking angry.

He pointed at me, as if to say, *Stay there.*

I don't think so. I moved away from the balcony and decided to take my chances down the hall to the right. I passed a giant home-theater room, a den or something like it, and a huge office—this Floyd dude was seriously loaded. At the end of the hall, there was a closed door. I reached for the handle and opened the door. I slipped inside the dark room and quickly closed it behind me.

That should save me from Ben for the moment, I thought. It took my eyes a few seconds to adjust to the darkness. I blinked, realizing I was in a bedroom of some kind. And in the back, there was a moving light.

A flashlight. *There was someone else here.*

11

THURSDAY, 7:55 P.M.

I FROZE. I REACHED BEHIND ME, LOWERing the door handle. I opened the door, but by then the flashlight was pointed right into my eyes.

I raised my hands to block out the light but was blinded all the same. I was about to speak up, when whoever wielded the flashlight shoved me out of the way and ran.

I blinked, but all I saw was a flash of someone's black loafers. There was a smell—like toothpaste—and I turned to follow, rubbing my eyes. "Wait up!" I called, knowing it was useless. I rushed past the theater room and the office, seeing spots the whole way.

Then I ran smack into Ben, who was beet red, he was so mad.

"Baker!" he hissed. "What are you doing here?"

"I'm on the case!" I pointed past him. "And this bad burglar dude just got away."

Ben looked where I pointed. "What are you talking about?"

"Never mind!" I rushed to the balcony and looked down. But it was no use. There were so many people, and I couldn't tell if any of them were wearing loafers—if that was even what I'd seen in my half-blind state.

Ben came up behind me. "You are not supposed to be here. You're compromising my cover!"

"I could say the same for you," I said, pointing at his bright shorts and I Love LA T-shirt. "You're like a glaring neon sign."

Ben clenched his jaw. "You must leave *now*. Albert Black said—"

"I don't care," I said, looking down below. A waiter was refilling the table of snacks. And that's when I saw a guy in black loafers. "Right there!" I called and pointed. "That's him." I looked over my shoulder at Ben, then at the long hallway that led to the stairs. If I went that way, I'd lose the bad dude again for sure.

I glanced over the balcony. Saw the chains, the ones that held up the table with snacks. My bad guy was just a few feet away from the buffet.

So I swung my right leg over the banister.

"Oh no you're not," Ben called behind me.

"Watch me," I said as I swung my left leg. From my spot

on the banister, I could reach the chain.

So I grabbed the cold metal with both hands.

And jumped.

I slid down the chain, feeling my palms burn as I landed on the table. And Ben followed on the chain at the other side of the table. He flew down with a terrified look on his face.

We both landed on our butts, me on some crackers with cheese, Ben on a bowl of egg salad. Needless to say, I got the better landing spot.

Not that I cared. I was chasing my bad dude in the loafers—Ethan Melais, I figured. But where did he go? A crowd of people gathered around us, looking shocked, a few laughing as Ben tried to wipe the egg salad from his pants. But as much as I enjoyed some Ben humiliation, I had a mission to accomplish.

I hopped off the table and pushed past the party guests, rushing toward the door—I even looked up toward the balcony again, to see if maybe he'd gone back up. But I just saw beautiful Savannah, shaking her head at the big mess downstairs.

My bad dude was gone.

"What's all this then?" Floyd sounded seriously miffed. I could see why: We'd just crashed his fancy party—literally. Behind Floyd stood a guy with slicked-down hair and wire-rimmed glasses. He had an earpiece and carried a tablet. Maybe his assistant or something.

I turned to look at Ben, who was giving me the stink eye. Me, I just wanted to find some napkins to wipe the cheese off my jeans. "Um . . . I'm sorry," I said. "I was leaning over your balcony and fell down."

"And who's this bloke?" Floyd pointed a chubby finger at Ben. Then he broke out in a huge grin. "Wait a minute . . . you've got a twin, and you didn't tell me." He laughed, and the party crowd fake-laughed with him.

This wasn't funny at all.

"He's not my twin," Ben snapped. He'd given up on getting his pants clean and was now standing in his trademark pose: legs shoulder-width apart, arms crossed.

I wanted Ben to shut up. This twin idea was obviously something Floyd liked. Why not roll with it? We'd just ruined the guy's egg salad, so we might as well keep ourselves out of trouble by pretending.

"Ben here doesn't like to be twins," I said, throwing my double a death-ray stare. Hoping he got the hint. "It makes him feel inferior, standing in my shadow," I added with a grin.

"I'm sure it does, Linc." Floyd nodded and looked over his shoulder at the guy with the tablet. "This is my assistant director, Larry."

The dude nodded.

Floyd said, "Don't you think this twin situation is brilliant, Larry?"

"Absolutely," Larry said, never taking his eyes off the tablet. "We can shoot longer days."

"Huh?"

"The movie, kid." Larry gave me an irritated look over his glasses. "Using twins gets us around child labor laws."

Floyd clapped his hands with glee. "It's settled. We'll see you two tomorrow on the set."

Of course, it wasn't exactly settled. Not at all. After getting contracts from Larry and a nine a.m. call time, Ben and I left the mess at Floyd's party, both smelling like funky food, and pretended to exit the mansion together.

But once we made it past the metal gate, we sprinted toward the van. I had to be first to explain this new development to Black and Stark—Ben would just blame it all on me. Even if it was sort of my fault.

As it turned out, Ben was still in much better shape than I was. He was already a dozen feet ahead of me, pulling at the van's sliding door, when I slowed down. By the time I caught up, I could hear him yelling at Stark.

"Amateur . . . disaster . . . chicken salad on my pants!" Ben's voice sounded kind of squeaky because he was so upset.

"It was *my* case first, you know," I said as I got into the van. "And you didn't have to jump off the balcony."

Black took a deep breath, the kind adults take when they're trying not to blow their top over something I did. I know this deep-breath thing well. "Didn't I kick you off the case?" Black hissed.

"Floyd showed up, offered to give me a ride to the party," I said, and shrugged. "What was I supposed to do?" I looked for a window to open, since Ben and I smelled kind of ripe. But the van's sliding door was it, and I wasn't about to open that one back up. Someone might just push me out. "And he was pretty happy about Ben and me looking alike." I told Black and Stark about me chasing that guy who had blinded me with the flashlight, and taking a jump off the balcony.

"Wait—back up a second," Stark said from the passenger seat. "You caught a guy breaking into one of Floyd's bedrooms?"

I nodded. "Yeah. But I couldn't really tell what he was doing—he had that flashlight in my face almost the whole time."

Stark inhaled sharply. "What did he look like?"

"I don't know, it was just some guy. Maybe it was Melais." I shrugged. "I almost caught him."

"*Almost* being the operative word," Ben said. "Instead, we're both wearing hors d'oeuvres."

"Orr—what?"

"Appetizers," Stark said.

"Oh," I said, feeling kind of dumb. "Well, at least I was on the job. And you guys were all ready to give the mission to by-the-book Ben here," I added, pointing at my look-alike.

"So how did you two get away after blowing your cover?" Black asked.

I told him about the twin stuff.

"That settles it." Black clapped his hands. "You're twins."

Ben and I started arguing at the same time.

"Silence—both of you!" Black put the van in drive. "Tomorrow, bright and early, you can get back to work. Find Ethan Melais. And get me that Dangerous Double."

12

PLACE: AUNT JENNY AND UNCLE TIM'S HOUSE

TIME: FRIDAY, 7:29 A.M.

STATUS: ASLEEP

"LINC!"

I made a moaning noise. Mornings are not my best time. And someone was slapping my face—gently, but still. Who wants to start the day that way?

"Wake up, kid."

"Huh!" I sat up, and took a split second to remember where I was. My aunt and uncle's place, sleeping on a fold-away bed. Bunking with Grandpa.

"Good, you're awake," Grandpa said. He was sitting on his bed, which was just a few inches away from mine. He smelled like old-dude cologne, and had his hair neatly brushed back in his usual fifties style. Grandpa is an early bird, unlike yours truly. He likes to be in and out of the shower, ready for breakfast and his crossword by seven a.m., even on weekends.

"What time is it, anyway?" I looked around for a clock, but there wasn't one. Just the usual small guest room, with framed posters of cars all around. Grandpa had opened the curtain, so bright sunlight was hurting my still-sleepy eyes.

"It's seven thirty—what does it matter!" Grandpa looked kind of panicky. He leaned close. "There's an enemy at the gates."

"What are you talking about?"

Now, Grandpa isn't going nuts or anything, in case that's what you're thinking. He can just be a little . . . paranoid. He thinks life is one big episode of the crime shows he likes. Last month, he thought the checkout girl at the supermarket was an undercover cop. He had this whole weird conversation with her, and gave her a detailed description of the poor produce guy, who Grandpa thought was a criminal.

"Grandpa," I moaned, and dropped back on my flimsy mattress. A coil poked at the bottom of my spine, so I sat up again.

Grandpa pointed out the window. "Out there, go see! There's a sinister woman watching the house."

That got my attention. What if it was that suspicious lady from yesterday, studying her map again?

I walked to the window and looked outside. There was a parked sedan, dark blue, obviously a rental. There was a woman in a black suit behind the wheel. Though I could only see part of her face, I knew it was Agent Stark. Probably waiting to give me a ride, or drop off a case file or whatever. "That's no enemy, Grandpa."

"7TRZ211," he said, reciting the plate, looking smug. "I have her details." He waved his notebook, the one where I knew he wrote down license plates and descriptions of dubious characters.

I looked outside and caught a glimpse of the back of her car. "That's not even the right plate, Grandpa. And this lady is just here to give me a ride to the movie lot."

Grandpa pushed me aside and peered out the window. "Oh, I thought I saw a different car," he muttered, sounding disappointed. He took off his glasses, rubbed them on his vest, and put them on again. "Never mind, then."

"No one messes with the Bakers, Grandpa." I got up. "I'm gonna take a shower, okay? She's one of the good guys."

After I got dressed, I grabbed my backpack and attached my skateboard with the Velcro straps. Then I went down to the kitchen for some breakfast to go, so I could catch up with Agent Stark before she got too cranky about having to wait for me. Fortunately, it was only Mom in the kitchen. Unfortunately, she was chopping onions, making the place reek like a middle-school gym right after PE.

"Off to the set already?" Mom asked. She was peeling another onion, making my stomach turn. It was eight o'clock—a little early for anything but cereal or eggs.

"The movie people sent a car."

"I'd prefer it if Mike drives you next time," Mom said, wiping her eyes. "And I really want to meet that director guy, once I get a handle on things here . . ."

"Why the onions in the morning?" I asked, changing the subject.

"Macaroni salad." She shook her head in frustration. "I can't seem to get the balance right on the dressing."

"Good luck with that." I rummaged inside the large pantry and found a breakfast bar for the road. "Oh, Grandpa needs new glasses."

"Again already?"

"Yeah. I think he's seeing things." I told her about the whole license-plate situation that morning.

Mom nodded. "We'll look into it next week. Go be a movie star."

"It's only a small part," I said. That was kind of true, since I had no plans to stick around once I got the hat and Melais.

"I left the signed contract over there." Mom pointed to the other side of the kitchen counter. "Call me at lunch, so I know where you are."

I grabbed my paperwork and rushed out the door before she could start asking questions. Thank goodness for her obsession with making the perfect macaroni salad for the reunion picnic. Outside, Dad and Aunt Jenny had their heads stuck under the rusty car's hood.

"How's it going?" I asked Uncle Tim, who stood at a distance on the lawn.

He made a face that told me things weren't looking so good. "We'll have to see."

Enough said. I felt guilty about taking off, but knew I had to get to the mission. I waved good-bye and made my way to the dark-blue rental car.

Agent Stark didn't seem mad at all—surprising, considering she'd been sitting there waiting.

"I didn't know you were driving me," I said, buckling my seat belt.

"I thought you might need a ride." Stark put the car in drive and pulled into the street. Why was she being so nice?

"I could've had Mike drive me to the studio."

"Didn't you look at your call sheet?"

Not that closely. But I wasn't about to admit that.

"Apparently, you're filming on location, at Grauman's Chinese Theatre." That was about half an hour from my aunt and uncle's place, depending on traffic. "Call time is nine a.m."

"I remembered that." I knew Stark was the quiet type, so I turned on the radio, hoping to break the silence.

But after we got onto the highway, Stark turned off the radio. "Did I ever tell you how I came to join Pandora?" She glanced over at me.

"No." Was Agent Stark about to spill her guts? This was weird. "You only told me that you were let go or something, right?"

"More like reassigned—only I didn't know it at the time." She exhaled, gripping the steering wheel. "There was a case.

The CIA sent me to Italy, to chase down a suspected information broker. A freelance spy."

"Ethan Melais."

"Exactly." Stark paused, like maybe she was trying to figure out how to tell the story.

"You were sent to Italy to catch Melais."

Stark nodded. "That photograph was of a hotel where several high-powered executives were meeting. Somehow, Melais managed to get inside. We got that image off the security cameras." Stark gripped the steering wheel even tighter. "I was outside the room, posing as hotel security, waiting for him to show up."

"But you didn't catch him."

Stark shook her head. "He managed to slip inside that meeting room, and . . ." She clenched her jaw.

"What did this Melais dude do?"

"He stole the plans to a top secret hideout for . . . never mind, it's not important. But afterward, he slipped his calling card inside my jacket pocket." Stark reached inside her jacket and handed me a black business card.

Ethan Melais was all it said, in fancy cream letters.

"Yikes," I mumbled. That was like sticking your tongue in someone's face. I handed the card back.

"Needless to say, my career with the CIA was over." Stark glanced at me. "But then I was reassigned to a black-ops team that was just getting started—so in a way, Pandora and Albert Black saved me. It's really important to me to catch the guy. For him to see my face when I cuff him."

"You want to get revenge," I said. I got it: Agent Stark had a score to settle.

"Not revenge, exactly. More like . . ." She was searching for the right words; I could tell by the wrinkles on her forehead.

"Set things right."

"Exactly!" Agent Stark gave me a crooked, worried smile. "So what I need you to do is call me first. If you catch him."

"*When* I catch him, you mean."

"Sure, when you catch him. Or if Ben does . . ." Her voice trailed. "I have faith in you." She forced a smile, which with Stark was never a pretty sight.

"It'll be me catching this Ethan Melais, you know." I realized I sounded like a cranky toddler, but I didn't care. "Ben's on my turf now. He won't make it in California. I'll show him who the real junior secret agent is."

I had my own score to settle, like Agent Stark. "I'll get Ethan Melais and the Dangerous Double. Just watch."

13

FRIDAY, 8:55 A.M.

I WAS SO BUSY IMAGINING HOW I WAS going to catch Ethan Melais and prove to everyone that I was a great junior secret agent, I didn't even register that we'd left the highway. We were now somewhere in downtown Los Angeles.

"Why stop here?" I asked when Stark put the car in park. We were in a creepy-looking alleyway. There were a couple of overflowing Dumpsters and a dirty white stucco wall. "I thought the movie was supposed to be shot at the Chinese Theatre."

"We're a block away," Stark said. "I have to leave you here, so we don't blow your cover."

That made sense. I opened my door and got out, still

feeling a little weird about the conversation. Also, the alley smelled kind of funky, so that didn't help things.

"Linc," Stark called, leaning on the passenger seat. "Keep this between us, all right? Don't tell Ben."

Like I was going to tell him anything. "Sure."

And Stark was off. Me, I was feeling a little stressed out at this point. I had to find Ethan Melais and the Dangerous Double, and save the city and my family. Oh, and on top of that, I had to act in a movie. Next to a pretty girl, no less.

No pressure.

I took my skateboard off my backpack and rode on the sidewalk. I was kind of nervous over the whole movie stuff, to tell you the truth.

I made my way to Hollywood Boulevard, and already it was busy with the usual pedestrian traffic. Tourists gawking at the sights. Some dude was taking a picture of the street sign and a palm tree. I gave up riding my board and walked the rest of the way. LA was pretty cool. I felt a rush of excitement—I was going to catch a bad guy, impress everyone.

Beat Ben Green.

As I got closer to the Chinese Theatre, I reached a big crowd. There was a roadblock made out of sawhorse barricades, and security guards dressed in navy blue were guarding the open street behind it. Floyd even got permission to block off the Chinese Theatre. This movie was a bigger deal than I thought.

I told one of the security guards who I was, and after he checked with someone over his earpiece, I got permission to pass. I strapped my skateboard to my backpack and walked toward a cluster of trailers. There were about ten or so of them, set up to create a U shape. Savannah was sitting on the small steps in front of one of the trailers. She was dressed like it was the 1920s or something: dark gray dress, hair in a long braid. She was eating an apple. And giving me the stink eye.

"If it isn't the one-hit wonder," Savannah said with a fake smile. Why did this girl hate my guts?

"Who messed with your cereal this morning?" I said, figuring I would give her a taste of her own medicine.

And that's when I saw the door of a red trailer open, a few spaces down from where Savannah sat. A kid came out, wearing pants and a white shirt with suspenders, hair messed up, smears of dirt on his face.

Ben Green. He beat me to the set.

He smirked. Then he made a big deal of checking his watch, only to realize he wasn't wearing one with his 1920s wardrobe. "Made it out of bed, did you, Baker?"

"We were supposed to start at nine, so I'm right on time, *Baker*," I hissed, reminding him of the cover, and that he was a Baker too.

Ben lowered his voice so no one could hear. "Larry phoned and told me the call time had been changed to zero eight hundred. He didn't notify you?"

"No he didn't! He probably thought you'd tell me, with us being twins and all."

Ben shrugged and gave me one of his annoying smirks.

Just then Larry, the assistant director, stalked over,

looking seriously angry. At me. "Call time was moved to eight, Linc."

"But I—"

Larry waved his hand in dismissal. "At least your brother is here on time. He already gave me his contract—you have yours, at least?"

I handed Larry my signed contract.

Larry snatched it from my hands and stuffed it in a big folder without looking at it. He turned to Ben. "We're shooting in five. You too, Savannah." And he stalked back the way he came.

Savannah walked over. The girl already hated my guts; I didn't need her to think I was a hothead too. I'd get Ben back later.

"Ready to start, Ben?" she asked.

"Absolutely."

"Wait," I said, almost pulling Savannah's arm but stopping myself. "You hate me, but he's your friend?"

"Ben spent three years with the Camden Acting Studio in London, and he told me that you never even passed the first round of auditions."

Ben gave me a triumphant grin.

"He may be doing you a favor, getting this part, but I know who *you* are." Savannah raised her left eyebrow and looked at me like I was a day-old bologna sandwich. "An amateur."

"We should go," Ben said, pulling her along. I think he knew I was about to lose my cool.

"Let's get to work." Savannah straightened her spine,

turned, and walked away, with Ben trailing along.

I'd been outplayed. By the dumbest junior secret agent ever, no less. Okay, maybe he wasn't the dumbest. It was a smart move, I had to admit.

I just had to be smarter.

Because while Ben was playing actor from the whatever studio in London, I would beat him where it mattered: figuring out who on the set was Ethan Melais. And I'd arrest him, and bring him to Stark. Then I'd get the Dangerous Double.

I looked around the area at the center of the trailers. There were a couple of people buzzing around. A dude with a clipboard, talking to a woman carrying a stack of papers. Another guy, carrying a tray of coffee cups, trying not to drop it. And Kate, the makeup artist I'd met at Floyd's party. She waved and gave me a smile before disappearing inside her trailer.

And that's when I spotted this guy leaning against the red trailer that was parked right next to Kate's. He had long curly hair and wore a faded brown fedora hat. The guy popped a piece of gum in his mouth and gave me a nod.

That red trailer was where Ben had come out, wearing his 1920s outfit. I'd bet it was the costume department on wheels. What better place to hide a Chaplin hat without arousing suspicion, right?

I made my way over. Let's face it: I had no leads, so the costume trailer was a good place to start.

"Gum?" the guy asked.

I shook my head. "No thanks."

"I'm Kurt." He put the gum pack back in his white shirt's breast pocket. He adjusted his fedora. "You're Linc, right?"

"Yeah." We shook hands.

"I saw you at Sterling yesterday, when those security guards busted you." He thumbed over his shoulder at the trailer. "I had just loaded her up out back."

The Dangerous Double! It had to be in there. But wait—did that mean this dude Kurt was Ethan Melais? I tried to picture him as Melais but was having a hard time.

"So Floyd cast you, but now your brother is out there," Kurt said, smacking his gum. "You're competitive, huh?"

"You have no idea."

"I get it. I have a brother who lives up in Seattle. He's an accountant. Always likes to remind me he makes more money than me."

This was fascinating, but I had to get to the case already. I glanced over Kurt's shoulder at the costume trailer. "You think I can have a tour?"

"Of the trailer?" Kurt shook his head. "Naw, wish I could. Got a guy coming for a fitting any minute now."

Behind him, I could see some boxes—even a couple of those fancy hatboxes. One of them could have the Dangerous Double inside! "Don't you have a costume for me?"

Kurt shook his head. "Only got one, since we didn't think we'd be having twins. I'm working on making a duplicate, but right now you're gonna have to swap with your brother at lunch. Once I finish your costume, maybe you can have a tour."

"No sweat." I would just have to come back later to check the place out. And once I found the hat, I'd have proof that Kurt was Ethan Melais.

This case turned out to be a breeze after all.

I said, "I'll go watch the set. You think that's okay?"

Kurt laughed. "Yeah. If you can handle it."

"What do you mean?"

"You'll see." He turned to go back inside his top secret trailer. "Let's just say Floyd lives up to his reputation. And then some. I'm glad I'm not an intern or a grip is all I'm getting at."

"A grip?"

"Those are the people who move stuff around on the set. Floyd will yell at them the loudest," Kurt said before he closed the door to his trailer.

I left and made my way between the trailers, toward the set. Several cameras were set up, and groups of movie-crew members hung back, watching the Chinese Theatre. I couldn't see the handprints by big movie actors in the concrete along the Hollywood Walk of Fame out front, but I knew they were there. Years ago, Mom and Dad took me for a trip here.

The theater itself looks exactly like what you'd think: Chinese, with a really tall pagoda-style entry. There are two lion statues on either side, and golden double doors that lead inside. It looks kind of ridiculous, if you want to know the truth. I mean, we're not in China, right?

Not that anyone cared: Behind the sawhorse barriers on the street, there were a few hundred people gawking, trying to snap pictures of the actors.

As I walked closer to the set, I saw Ben and Savannah standing on the road, next to the red carpet that ran to the theater entrance. Ben looked nervous and kind of pale, like he was ready to lose his breakfast.

"No, no, NO!" That was Nigel Floyd, having a fit. He shook his head.

I stopped—let's face it: Normally, if there was a grown-up yelling, it was at me. So for once, I was happy to be out of range.

Floyd pointed his finger at Ben. "You've got it all wrong. ALL. WRONG!"

Ben looked shocked, and a little angry. But he didn't say anything. Savannah took a step to the left, and another, distancing herself from Ben.

"You studied at Camden Studios in London? My foot!" Floyd was practically spitting at Ben now. I actually felt bad—but only a little.

"Sir, you need to calm down now," Ben tried. His voice trembled.

But that only fueled Floyd's fire. "I need to do no such thing, you little . . ." He waved, until his assistant director, Larry, appeared at his side. "Get him OFF MY SET!"

"You got it, Nigel," Larry said, not looking at all stressed out. He was obviously used to these outbursts. Larry tried to grab Ben by the elbow.

But Ben pulled away. He looked like he was about to blow up—I'd never seen him this mad.

They passed me, and Larry brushed my shoulder. He smelled faintly of something chemical—toothpaste, or mints? "You're up, kid," he said.

I turned and watched Larry walk away, expecting me to follow. The hair on the back of my neck stood up.

Was Larry actually Ethan Melais?

FRIDAY, 9:30 A.M.

I WAS ABOUT TO CHASE AFTER LARRY, when Floyd motioned me over. "You!"

I froze. My suspect was getting away!

"Lincoln Baker," Floyd called. "Get yourself over here."

I walked over, feeling like all the tourists at the barricades were staring at me. "Me? But I thought you had Ben."

"Ben *reeeeally* stank," Savannah muttered under her breath as I passed.

Floyd held me by the shoulders, squeezing me like my aunt Jenny likes to do. "I always knew you were the real talent here." He smiled. "Get dressed; you're up."

"Okay."

"EVERYONE!" Floyd hollered. "TAKE FIFTEEN!" Then

he waved his hand in a circular motion. "And Larry."

"Yes," Larry said right next to me. This dude was like a ninja—and now another suspect as Ethan Melais.

"Get these barriers pushed back before I kill me some tourists."

"Yes, Nigel."

Floyd stalked away, leaving me with Larry. Savannah was smart and had disappeared.

"Come with me," Larry said without looking at me. "Go see Kurt in costume and Kate for makeup. Be back in ten minutes, or you're next to be axed." And he walked away. Nice, these Hollywood people.

But at least Ben was out of the picture—literally.

I made my way back to the trailers and almost got run down by Ben. He was back in his airport gift-shop outfit and shoved a bundle of clothes in my hands. "There's only one costume for now, since they weren't prepared for twins," he said, repeating what Kurt had told me earlier. "Take it, Baker." He gave me a death-ray stare and then shoved me in the shoulder as he walked away.

"I can't help it that I'm a better actor than you," I called at Ben's back. Not that I actually knew that for sure, but I couldn't possibly be as bad at it as Ben. Right?

Behind me, Kurt came out of the costume trailer and locked the door. So much for a chance to get inside and look for the Dangerous Double. This mission was turning from a breeze into a thunderstorm in a hurry.

"What are you still doing here, man?" Kurt asked me. He

pointed to a small white trailer parked across from his. "Go see Kate. You don't want to get Floyd mad."

"Everybody just chill already," I mumbled to myself. But I did hurry over to Kate's trailer, where I found her waiting for me near a chair that looked like the one in the dentist's office.

"Have a seat," she said.

I dropped my backpack on the floor and sat down, holding the pile of clothes Ben had given me on my lap. "Is this movie stuff always so stressful?" I asked as Kate smeared tan makeup on my cheeks and forehead.

"Not always." She worked quickly, covering my face and neck. "It depends on the director. Floyd likes things his way."

"No kidding."

She stepped back and nodded. "That'll do. You can change in here if you want; I'll step outside." Kate checked her watch. "You have five minutes to get back to the set, so you better hurry."

"I know, I know." I waited for her to leave and then quickly changed into my costume. I stuffed my shoes, jeans, and shirt inside my backpack. The costume pants were scratchy, and the suspenders cut into my shoulders. Plus, this makeup kind of smelled and felt like when your mom makes you wear five pounds of sunscreen. It was a good thing this movie was only a temporary gig. As soon as I caught Ethan Melais and got my hands on the Dangerous Double, I was out of here.

I hurried outside, passing Kate and Kurt, who were having some kind of serious discussion I wasn't going to stick around for. I made it to the set just as Larry handed Floyd a stack of papers.

"Great, you're here." Floyd looked up, and seemed happy to find that the barricades had been pushed back. No more nosy tourists. "Let's get started, everyone!"

Savannah was standing near the red carpet, and straightened when Floyd motioned for her to come over.

"Linc and Savannah, you're over there." Floyd motioned to the spot Savannah came from. "Maybe you'll be able to get this right instead of your untalented brother."

Larry let out a small laugh behind Floyd. Even though I hated Ben, I thought that was mean.

"So what are our lines?" I asked.

Which got me the stink eye from Floyd. "You have no lines."

Savannah snickered.

"Why not?" I asked. It was a valid question, right? I mean, wasn't I supposed to be the star here and everything?

"It's an *homage* to silent movies," Savannah said, sounding like my English teacher when I flunked a test. "None of us speak. Didn't you see that there's no boom man?"

"What's a boom man?"

"The guy holding the microphone—never mind."

Floyd waved his hand to our spot. "You're at a movie premiere. Just stand over there and watch the people on the red carpet."

That seemed easy enough. And I got to stand next to Savannah, which was pretty nice, even if she did hate me.

"How did Ben mess this up anyway?" I whispered, as Floyd walked away to talk to someone inside the parked car. "I mean, all he had to do was stand here."

Savannah sighed. "It's more than just standing. You have to imagine what your character *feels* in the moment. 'We think too much and feel too little'—that's what Chaplin said."

I still didn't get it. "We're just standing here. Maybe his feet were tired?"

"Never mind," Savannah said, and straightened. She closed her eyes, obviously concentrating.

Everyone in Hollywood is a nut job. You agree with me, right?

"Quiet on the set!" Larry called. Not that it was very noisy or anything—I mean, we didn't even have any lines.

"*The Hollywood Kid*, take six," some lady I couldn't see called.

I had no idea what I was supposed to do. Not that it mattered, because I noticed something else. The tourists, far off behind the barricades, were pointing—only not at us, but down the street. A few of them were taking pictures.

I looked to my left, to where this big guy was pointing. Past Savannah, who was busy looking sad. The crowd parted; some people were screaming.

And I saw this speeding red car. Heading straight for us.

15

FRIDAY, 10:01 A.M.

AT THAT MOMENT, I DIDN'T THINK. I grabbed Savannah and pushed her aside. She landed a few feet away, on her behind.

And the red car kept moving toward me—even though there was no driver behind the wheel. I stepped back just in time so I wouldn't get hit.

The car kept going, until it crashed into the building, where it died on the spot. Smoke came from the crumpled hood.

"What was that?" Savannah said as she got up next to me.

"A runaway car," I said, like it wasn't obvious. The crowd behind the barricades was roaring, and seemed to be applauding, for some reason.

Floyd looked shocked. "What the—" He said some four-letter words that I won't repeat—let's just say he was madder than my parents on report-card day.

A couple of security guards ran from inside the Chinese Theatre, looking at the building and the damage the car had caused. One of the guys threw his hands in the air.

"Oh no," Savannah said. "The theater . . ."

"We almost got hit by a speeding car," I said. "Who cares about the building?"

Savannah gave me a shocked look. "This is the Chinese Theatre we're talking about," she said, like I was supposed to get it now. "The Oscars will be held here Sunday. It was built in 1927—it's a movie-history landmark!" Savannah was trembling.

So I let it go, since one of the camera guys was already calling the police. I walked over to the car, where Larry and Floyd were checking out the exterior of the theater. Of course the car was empty.

"How did it even drive here?" Savannah asked.

I peered inside, and saw something wedged against the gas pedal. It took me a second to realize what it was. "A coat hanger," I said, more to myself than anyone else.

"Why would anyone stick a coat hanger against the gas pedal?" Savannah asked me.

"I don't know," I lied. Because I did know what this was about.

Ethan Melais. I'd bet my Xbox and all my games that he knew Pandora was on his tail. This car was meant to hit me.

Ethan Melais was trying to protect his identity, and the Dangerous Double.

The good news: This close call with a car bumper meant that I was hot on Melais's tail.

The bad news: Melais was willing to kill me to keep his identity a secret and use the Dangerous Double on Monday to get that drone-system prototype for the terrorists.

This case had just gotten really dangerous.

The police showed up a few minutes later and taped off the area. After they questioned Floyd and the cameraman, Larry managed to get the rest of the cast and crew out of there about an hour later without giving a statement or anything. Talking to the police might get sticky, with me working for Pandora and all, so I was happy to scram. The set was closed, and people were gathering equipment and hitching trailers to trucks, ready to go to the next location, which apparently was at the beach.

"That was scary," Savannah said as we walked back to the trailers. "Thank you."

"For what?"

"Saving me." She laughed. "You did shove me out of the way on purpose, didn't you?"

"Yeah, I did." I guess that kind of made me a hero. That had to be a good thing with pretty girls, right?

"Well, I owe you one," Savannah said, giving me the nicest smile in the whole world. She turned to walk the other way, probably to catch a ride or answer fan mail or something.

"Wait," I said, not wanting her to walk away. "Maybe you can help me."

She stopped. "Anything you want."

I swallowed. Why was this girl making me so nervous? "You're right: I have no idea what I'm doing here." I felt my face flush. I hoped Savannah didn't notice. "Can you help me? You know, with the acting and stuff?"

"Sure." She smiled. "You'll be fine. Floyd is an unconventional director. He just goes to the set and waits for inspiration to strike, like Charlie Chaplin used to do. Basically, he flies by the seat of his pants," Savannah added with a laugh.

That was pretty much my approach to Pandora missions, so I could relate. "I like that." I laughed, and it sounded weird, like I was nervous or something.

But Savannah didn't seem to notice. "If you want, I can give you a ride to the next location."

"Sure," I said. "But aren't you a little young to have a car?"

"What did you think—that I'd take the bus?" She laughed. "I have a driver, silly."

Of course she did. This was Hollywood.

"We'll head out after lunch, at noon. I'll see you then." Savannah smiled, and she was off.

"Savannah's nice, huh?"

I turned, only to look at my mirror image in a lame I Love LA shirt. "What are you still doing here, Ben? Didn't Floyd kick you off the set?"

"For now." Ben crossed his arms. "You are forgetting the objective here, Baker."

"Identify Ethan Melais and retrieve the Dangerous Double—I remember just fine." I was about to tell him about the incident with the runaway car but then changed my mind. I didn't want to give him the advantage. Because there was a clue, one that might reveal Ethan Melais's identity. And I wasn't about to share it with Ben.

"Well, you're getting some help on the mission," Ben said. "Your little friend Henry is here with his gadgets."

"Henry is here?" I suddenly felt a whole lot better. Henry is this brilliant kid who invents these super-handy gadgets for Pandora so I can ward off the bad dudes. Henry is a genius, and also a really great friend.

"He's inside that crepe stand." Ben pointed past the trailers, where a camper converted into a food truck was parked. Crepes-to-Go, it said on the side. The serving window was closed, which was a bummer, because I was pretty hungry. Around us, everyone was packing up to move to the next location. "I'll leave you to it," Ben said with a nod. He started walking off, and I actually felt a little bad for him.

"You can come," I said, regretting it as I spoke. I mean, I hated the guy.

Ben stopped and turned. He shook his head. "I don't have time for extracurricular activities. I have a lead to follow up on." What a windbag.

"You have a lead?" I asked.

Ben just gave me a half smile. "Good luck with your gadgets." He turned and walked away.

Whatever, I thought as I walked over to the food truck.

I had a lead of my own. Because the red runaway car that Melais sent to kill me had a clue: that clothes hanger. Ethan Melais could be the costume designer, Kurt.

Of course there was Larry—he was a good suspect too. Smelling minty, just like that dude who broke into one of Floyd's bedrooms.

But the clothes hanger was the strongest clue right now. So Kurt was suspect number one, with Larry as a backup. Now all I needed was proof—the Dangerous Double. And Henry's inventions would help me find it, and catch the bad guy, no doubt.

I was so caught up in my thoughts that it wasn't until I reached the Crepes-to-Go truck that I spotted someone out of the corner of my eye. A person, behind me, trailing me—I could feel it in my gut now, too. Like at school, when someone is trying to cheat off your paper or something.

I was being followed. I turned around, *fast.*

And stared right at my stalker.

16

FRIDAY, 11:45 A.M.

OKAY, SO MAYBE THIS PERSON WASN'T a stalker, *exactly*. It was just Kate.

"I'm sorry—I didn't mean to scare you." She laughed and handed me my backpack. "You left this in my trailer."

I took my backpack and realized my hands were shaking a little. Clipped to my bag, Dad's compass bounced around, sending the dial spinning. "Jeez, you're like a ninja."

"I try," Kate joked. Then her face got serious. "Are you okay? I heard about the runaway car on the set."

I nodded, and put on my backpack. "I'm fine. Probably just an accident," I lied.

"Are you sure about that?"

"Sure, yeah."

Kate nodded, but she looked worried. "Nigel brushed it

off so easily, but you could've gotten killed, Linc!"

Like I needed reminding. "So I guess we're moving to another location?" I asked, changing the subject.

Kate nodded, and checked her watch. "Better get a move on." She stepped back and smiled. "Just don't hesitate to ask if you need help, okay, Linc?"

"Sure."

"Enjoy the crepes. I'll see you on the beach."

"Yeah, sure." As nice as the beach might sound, I couldn't wait until this mission was done. I waited for Kate to be out of sight before opening the door.

Inside the food truck, the kitchen showed no signs of crepes being cooked, unfortunately for me and my growling stomach. Stark looked up from the tiny counter, where she had a map of the US spread out. She gave me a little nod. Black didn't even move his eyes away from the map. He looked even grumpier than normal.

But I didn't worry about him. Because to the left of the kitchen was a banquette, and sitting on one of the benches was my pal Henry. He jumped up when he saw me. "Linc!"

I tossed my backpack aside. We fist-bumped, and then he gave me a hug. Henry doesn't care much about being cool, which makes him the coolest guy I know.

"So good to see you, man," I said. There was a black backpack on the small table, and I pointed to it as I sat on the bench across from him. "What's this?"

Henry grinned. "Gadgets for you." He wiggled his freckled nose to push his black plastic-framed glasses up. "But first, I want you to tell me what it's like to be in the movies."

"It's just . . . weird," I said, and shrugged.

"That's all you've got?" Henry sounded disappointed.

"I've only been in one scene, and it got pretty messed up." I told him about the runaway car, and how it almost hit Savannah and me.

"You think someone did that on purpose?" Henry whispered.

"No one wedges a hanger against a gas pedal by accident," I said. "So yeah."

"Ethan Melais is trying to kill you—that's bad news. What if he succeeds?" Henry mused. His thinking out loud was not helpful. "Do you have a list of suspects?"

I told Henry about my suspicions of Kurt having the hat, and how with the clothes hanger being used, he was obviously Ethan Melais.

"Sounds like you already have your bad guy. You don't need my help." Henry looked defeated.

"I always need a gadget."

Henry perked up.

"Let's see them," I said, trying to sound enthusiastic. Truth was, Henry's gadgets had saved me more than once on these unpredictable Pandora missions. So I was really happy he was here.

Henry reached inside the backpack and pulled out a wooden box. He opened it and took out a black watch. "I know this looks kind of boring, but Agent Stark wouldn't let me pick a colorful one to modify." Stark was too busy talking to Albert Black to hear us. Henry leaned on the table to show me the face of the watch. "There's a button on the side, see?

Normally, you would use it as a stopwatch. But I made it so it deploys a bulletproof force field."

"No way!" I tried to reach over to touch the watch, but Henry pulled away.

"It only works if you push the button twice, and you can only use it once. Got it?" He gave me an urgent stare.

"Push button twice, use it once—got it," I said.

"Your bulletproof force field is three square feet, and it only lasts thirty seconds, so . . ."

"If I get shot at, I should scram in a hurry." I couldn't believe I just said that. Dudes shooting at me? That was the stuff of Grandpa's crime shows. "Hopefully, I won't need it."

"I call it the Three-by-Thirty—get it?" Henry likes to name his gadgets—it's a little silly, but sort of fun, too.

It took me a moment, but then I got it. "Three square feet, thirty seconds—Three-by-Thirty, of course."

"I should really get my work patented," Henry mused. He put the watch back inside the box and reached inside the backpack again. He showed me two long plastic straps.

"These look like those magnetic-bracelet things," I said. I'd seen the girls have them at school. You snap them over your wrist.

Henry nodded. "Except that if you slap these bracelets around someone's wrists, they click together and become a super magnetic cuff." He straightened. "I call it the Instacuff."

"Won't they go off by accident?"

"You have to snap them pretty hard," Henry said. Then he grinned. "I'll put them in the front pouch, to be safe."

"Smart." I was really good at getting into trouble. Last

thing I needed was to cuff myself during this mission.

"I made you two Instacuffs, in case you have extra bad dudes. You can undo them with two magnets on either side of the cuffs—I'll put them in here too, okay?" Henry put the Instacuffs and the magnets in the front pouch.

"Thanks, Henry."

"Also, I brought an old favorite." Henry dug inside the backpack and pulled out a small tablet, like an iPad, one I recognized from my first mission.

"The Double Detector." The tablet camera scans the area and finds items that are a certain temperature—twenty-point-two degrees Celsius. During our mission in Paris, Henry had found that that was the heat signature of a Dangerous Double. "The Double Detector will come in handy. It seems like this town is full of Charlie Chaplin bowler hats."

"I heard you found one at Sterling Studios," Henry said.

I flustered. "Yeah, that was kind of embarrassing. It was made in China."

Henry shrugged. "Honest mistake." He always knew how to make me feel better. "Oh, and I have one more gadget for you." He zippered the backpack and slid it across the table. "Lift it."

I did. It weighed next to nothing. "Whoa, what's this made out of?"

Henry smiled. "I developed a new fabric, with tiny helium bubbles in it. The backpack can be a flotation device—pretty cool, huh?"

"Very cool. And you added straps for my skateboard."

"Wouldn't let you leave home without your board, Linc.

Now all I need is a name for the fabric. . . ." Henry sat back, musing.

Albert Black folded the map and came over to the table. "I see you two are all done getting geared up. Now I want an update on this car crash. I saw the police and heard the crew talking. I want your side of the story."

I told him about the runaway car. "It has to be Ethan Melais—he knows I'm onto him. So now he's trying to kill me to protect his identity and keep the Dangerous Double." As I said those words, I felt a little droplet of sweat go down my back. This was serious business.

"Good," Albert Black said, leaning on the small table.

"Good?" I thought I was hearing things. "Someone tries to kill me, and you think this is a good thing—seriously?"

"Put some pressure on the guy. If he's panicking, he's more likely to expose his identity." Black grinned. "Maybe you can spread the word that you know who he is. Maybe he'll come after you again, so we can catch him. Set a trap."

Stark frowned behind him as she tucked some papers in a file, but didn't speak up.

"Back to work, kids." Black stood. "Henry will be looking at the security footage from Sterling Studios, see if he can spot Ethan Melais stealing the Dangerous Double. Maybe we can identify him."

"They just gave you the footage?" I asked.

Henry snickered. "No need. We're borrowing it from their computers."

"You hacked in? Nice," I said. Henry had more talents than I realized.

"I didn't get into their system yet, but I should have access in no time," Henry said, cracking his knuckles.

"And you'll be making crepes?" I said to Stark and Black.

"This is just a cover, kid, so we can hang around the set," Black said with a dark look. "I only reheat stuff in the microwave. You, Stark?"

"Strictly takeout, sir," Stark said with a nod. To me: "Agent Black and I will be coordinating the relocation of the other artifacts."

"Why?" I asked.

Stark gave me a tired and worried look. "With the Chaplin hat unsecured, we can't take any chances. We have to make arrangements to hide Pandora's other Dangerous Doubles from our warehouse."

This was the first I was hearing of a warehouse. "How many Doubles are there? And where's this warehouse?"

Black slapped the table. "That's not your concern. Let's just say there are more than ten and less than a thousand."

I almost rolled my eyes, but figured that would just get me into trouble.

"And the warehouse location is top secret," Black went on, "but with so many dangerous artifacts in one place, we can't risk Melais getting in with the Chaplin hat."

"The Einstein time-travel vortex in a jar alone . . . ," Stark mumbled.

Black slapped the table again and gave her the stink eye. "Point is, we'll be busy. Too busy to chase this con man. And since you managed to get cast in the movie, you have the best chance of catching the guy. So you need to find

Ethan Melais and the Chaplin hat."

I got up. "Okay, I guess I better get to the next shooting location." I transferred my stuff to my new super lightweight backpack. I strapped in my board and clipped Dad's compass to it. The new backpack felt strange, like it belonged to a real junior secret agent, not a regular kid like me.

"Watch your back," Stark said as I left the Crepes-to-Go trailer. "Melais is ruthless." She closed the door before I could respond.

"Thanks for the tip," I said to no one. I adjusted my new backpack's straps, checked my phone, and realized I was late for my ride with Savannah to get to the set. That's when I spotted her, standing near a bright white Cadillac.

"There you are!" she said. "I've been waiting here forever."

"Sorry."

"Come on, get in." Savannah opened the passenger door and got in first, sliding across the seat so I could join her. "Those crepes must be good."

I laughed. "Yeah. They're the stuff of legend." Then I realized: I never ate lunch. This was going to be a long afternoon.

There was a guy in the driver's seat, wearing a black suit. I buckled my seat belt as we pulled away from the trailer and passed a blue car. It was a compact that looked familiar, but it took me a second to realize.

It was the woman I saw yesterday. The lady with the short silver hair—she was fake-studying her map. Again.

I craned my neck to look out the back window. Just in time to lock eyes with the lady.

What was she doing here?

17

FRIDAY, 12:20 P.M.

THERE WASN'T ANYTHING I COULD DO AT that point—I mean, Savannah's driver was punching the gas and ran a red light. So I turned back around in my seat.

"Are you okay?" Savannah asked.

"Yeah. Just thought I saw someone I recognized." I had a nagging feeling in my gut. Who was this lady, and what did she want?

"I owe you an apology," Savannah said.

"For what?

She looked uncomfortable. "I'm sorry I was so rude to you before, at the trailers this morning? I just . . ."

"You've been working on your acting a long time—I get it. I'm just some kid crashing the party."

She sighed. "Now you sound like me. Let me make it up to you—would you come to the Hollywood Bowl tomorrow night? I'm performing at this celebration to commemorate music and cinema for Academy Awards weekend. I'll get you a good seat."

"Sure. I mean, I'd love to." The Hollywood Bowl is only the coolest place to see a concert in the whole country. And being invited by Savannah made it even better.

"I got this great costume, totally authentic-looking—Kurt helped me put it together yesterday. And Kate said she'd do my makeup."

"I'll be there."

Because of an accident on the I-10, the driver took Santa Monica Boulevard. We passed all the usual tourist highlights: the fancy stores, the palm trees, and Beverly Hills, of course. Only it took forever, because we got stuck at every light.

Not that I cared. Being in a car with Savannah was okay with me: She was pretty nice, and it meant I didn't have to ride with Ben or in the crepe truck or something.

Savannah asked, "Do you know anything about cinema history?"

Um, no. But I didn't want to seem like I never paid attention in school, even if that was sort of the truth. I said, "I was hoping you might help me with that. What's *The Hollywood Kid* even about? Kate tried to explain it to me before, but . . . I guess I'm too much of a new kid on the set to get it."

Savannah laughed. She snorted, too, but it was sort of cute. "Have you ever watched any silent movies, like the ones made by Charlie Chaplin, Buster Keaton, and Harold Lloyd?"

I shook my head. Might as well be honest, since she seemed to like me better now. "We watch a lot of crime shows at my house." I told her about Grandpa and his obsession with cops and bad dudes. "And we watch the History Channel when Dad's around. He loves that, although he usually falls asleep about ten minutes into the show. Otherwise I play video games and hang out with my friends."

She actually looked a little envious. "My father is a musical composer for movies and TV shows. My mom is an actress—Ava Stone?"

"You're her daughter?" Ava Stone is one of the most famous actresses of all time. "My mom loves her. I bet you're an expert on movies."

She smiled. "Pretty much. I've seen all of the silent-movie classics—and I watched them again to prepare for this role. It's a whole different kind of acting when you can't use dialogue."

"Sure, yeah." I had no idea what she meant, of course.

"*The Hollywood Kid* is all about showing the silent movie in contrast to modern life—isn't it a brilliant concept?" Savannah seemed super excited about it. "To demonstrate the power of that silence, to show not tell. I love it."

"Floyd doesn't seem too happy about how things are going," I said. Outside, we passed a cluster of tourists taking pictures of the Beverly Hills sign. "Did he even get any footage at the Chinese Theatre?"

"Some. Your brother was making it really hard. Ben just

doesn't have any charisma." Savannah flustered. "I'm sorry, I'm totally being rude."

"No worries," I said. "We don't exactly get along."

"He's very different from you." Savannah studied my face, making me feel really uncomfortable. "Like you're not even related."

"So is Floyd always this grumpy?" I asked, hoping to talk about something else.

Savannah laughed. "He can get much worse. Nigel is just a perfectionist—much like Chaplin, if you think of it." Her face darkened. "But lately, I don't know . . ."

"What?"

"Nigel seems very stressed out. He can't seem to focus. . . ." She paused. "I caught a conversation with his assistant director. I think there are some funding issues."

So Floyd was broke. This added an interesting angle that might help me with the case. They needed money for this movie. Having the Dangerous Double to steal that drone-system prototype would be like hitting the jackpot.

Maybe Larry should move to the number one spot as my prime suspect. Or Floyd.

"We barely shot footage at the theater, and now we're changing set location in the middle of the day." Savannah bit her lip. "It's weird."

"How so?"

"Normally, Floyd does a bunch of different takes—like Chaplin, he's famous for it. But right now, it's like he's not focused." She shrugged. "Maybe this set will be better."

We'd arrived at the parking area near the beach now, and I was sorry I had to get out. It was pretty nice to hang with Savannah, without all the Pandora mission and movie stress, or stupid Ben getting in the way. I lingered, pretending to mess with the straps of my backpack.

"I just want to stay in the car, don't you?" Savannah said. "See that wind blow? The water has to be freezing." She rubbed her arms, imagining the chill. "I'm not looking forward to this scene."

"Wait—we have to get into the water?"

"It's a vignette featuring Harold Lloyd's *By the Sad Sea Waves*—didn't they tell you?"

Of course they didn't. Not that it mattered so much, because I didn't know what that movie was about anyway.

Savannah opened the car door, letting in a waft of chilly air. "We don't just have to get into the water—we have to swim in it."

In February, in the freezing Pacific? That was not good.

"And with Floyd doing thirty, forty takes . . ." Savannah frowned as she looked at the choppy waves. "That's a few hours in the water, at least."

I groaned and got out of the car. The wind felt even colder than earlier. And I was hungry, too, which made me feel even colder.

A giant wave crashed on the sand. We would freeze to death out there. And with Melais on my tail, who knew what was going to happen?

I swallowed as I thought of the cold water.

I should probably mention that I'm not exactly the world's best swimmer. I know that sounds kind of weird coming from a California kid, but it's the truth. I had my swimming lessons and did all right, but I was never the guy to feel like going surfing or anything like that. I'm more of a skateboarder, video gamer—you get the idea.

So now I had to go wade into the Pacific and do whatever Floyd told me to?

No thanks.

It looked like they were already setting up to shoot the movie, with trailers in the familiar U shape.

To make matters worse, I spotted Ben. He'd caught a ride on the crew bus and was getting off. While I'd be floating in the freezing Pacific, he'd find Ethan Melais and the Dangerous Double.

I groaned.

Then I had an idea. What if I was the one chasing down that dangerous Chaplin hat and cuffing Ethan Melais for Agent Stark? What if it wasn't me, but Ben in the water . . . ?

"Linc Baker!" I heard Floyd call behind me. "Get ready to shoot."

I turned and smiled. "Not me, sir. I'm Ben. You want him, over there."

Ben looked up, confused. "Me?"

I said, "He's the one you want—my brother. Linc Baker."

18

FRIDAY, 1:15 P.M.

BEN PASSED ME AND WHISPERED, "WHAT are you doing, Baker?"

"I can't swim," I said. Okay, so maybe that was stretching the truth a little. But if Floyd stuck me in the freezing Pacific for hours, I'd never make it. "Can you just go with it?"

Ben looked toward the set, and I saw his eyes rest on Savannah, who was waiting for directions. "Okay," he said. "But don't go causing trouble, messing up the case."

"When have I ever done that?"

Ben gave me an eye roll, and then took off toward Floyd and the set. I watched Kurt hand him a costume, so at least I didn't have to change out of mine. Much as I hated to see my overeager look-alike steal the spotlight, I had to focus on the case. Before Ben could catch Melais and get the Dangerous Double. And before someone expected me to do any real acting.

But first, I had to call home.

"Are they feeding you lunch over there?" Mom asked. She's really into nutrition, and usually packs me a lunch with all the food groups represented.

"Oh yeah," I lied. "Healthy sandwiches and juice."

"Good. Is it fun?"

"Loads," I said, lying some more.

"You sound worried," Mom said. She had her mom radar going, even through the phone. "Are they being nice to you?"

I thought of the near miss with that runaway car. "It's Hollywood, Mom."

"Do we need to come get you, Linc?"

I reminded myself of the mission. The drone-system prototype, and how this Melais dude would sell it to that terrorist group if I didn't find the Dangerous Double. I had to stay on the case, to keep my family safe. "I can handle myself, Mom."

"I know. When are you done with this movie?"

"By Sunday, at the latest. I'll be there for the barbecue." One way or another, by Monday nine a.m. this case would be decided. And we were scheduled to drive back from the reunion on Sunday night. So if I was going to prove Pandora wrong, and show everyone I could do more than just get into trouble, I had to get moving. Catch Melais. Get the Dangerous Double.

I hung up after promising to be home by dinner. Then I

made my way over to the trailers. There was a group of people, and it looked like they were angry about something. One dude was waving a stack of paper, saying something about a contract. Thankfully, they disappeared toward the set.

Because I spotted the costume trailer. I rushed over and walked up the steps. Tried the door handle. It was unlocked!

I couldn't believe my luck. I peered around the door. "Kurt?"

Nothing. The trailer was deserted. So I snuck inside and closed the door. Kurt had a small sitting area at the front, and racks of clothing on either side in the middle of the trailer. Toward the back, there was a small kitchen with a table and benches across it, and past that a half-open curtain. I imagined people might get dressed back there or something.

I scoured the sitting area, passed the clothes racks, and focused on the kitchenette next. I opened some cabinets, but it was all plastic cups, crackers, and other random snack-type stuff. I ignored my growling stomach—I was on the clock here. If Kurt came back, I'd be in real trouble.

Since the kitchenette was a bust, I tried the table behind me. This looked more promising: There were stacks of paper, some that looked like script pages and others like printed memos. But then I spotted a white box, shoved in the corner of the bench. *Receipts*, it read on the side, and I felt my hopes sink. But it was all I had right now, so I opened it. Looked inside.

Inside there were—you guessed it—receipts. I riffled through them anyway, feeling like I might be better off eating some of those crackers to shut up my stomach, when I spotted something.

A boarding pass. It said LAX—I knew that was the airport code for Los Angeles—to FRA. I read the ticket, and saw the destination.

Frankfurt. Stark had mentioned there had been a Melais theft there. Kurt was Ethan Melais!

"Yesss," I said to myself, because this was good news. I caught the bad guy; now I could focus on finding that Chaplin hat.

Only then I heard the trailer door open.

I was busted, again.

19

FRIDAY, 1:33 P.M.

"KURT?" KATE STOOD IN THE DOORWAY, and spotted me. She froze. "Linc?"

"No, it's Ben. I was looking for Kurt too," I said, quickly stuffing the boarding pass in my back pocket. I pushed the box back with my knee. "Thought he might be back here taking a nap or something."

Kate studied me, like she was making up her mind.

"Kurt's not here." I walked toward her, hoping I could scram already. This trailer was feeling very hot and stuffy all of a sudden.

"I came to get him for the set, but we must've passed each other," Kate said. "What did you need him for anyway?"

"Um, Linc had a wardrobe issue, but no biggie." I was grateful for the cold air.

"Let's go to the set," Kate said. "Tons of touch-up to do with these water scenes."

"Sure, yeah." What I really wanted to do was call Agent Stark about this new lead, but it would just have to wait.

"So how do you like the work so far?" Kate asked as we walked between two trailers.

"You mean acting?"

She laughed. "What else would there be?"

You have no idea, lady. "It's okay. I only wish I could be as good as Linc." I couldn't help myself, what can I say.

"Hmmm, yes, he's quite the character. I imagine you bring your own talents to the table, though," she added.

"Not really." We were getting closer to the beach and the set. One camera was set up on the sand, and one on a boat, a little ways out in the water. I did a double take.

The boat was sinking.

I could see Savannah, on the sinking boat. She was soaked, and the camera dude looked totally lost.

Where was Ben?

Off in the distance, I spotted him. Or his head anyway. He was bobbing in the water; then he tried to swim to the shore, but was making no headway.

"Somebody call the coast guard!" Floyd hollered. He looked like he was losing it.

Larry was busy dialing on his phone, and so were a few other people.

"Where are the lifeguards?" Floyd asked no one in particular.

Larry answered, "You sent them away, remember?"

Floyd looked confused.

"That boat is the only one we have," Kate said next to me. She covered her mouth, looking really worried.

Ben was trying to swim to shore again, but just kept drifting farther back.

"He's caught in the current," I said to Kate. "Don't they have a backup boat, or a helicopter or something?"

Kate shook her head. "The budget is blown as it is. We're cutting corners where we can," she said, her voice drifting. "Is Linc a good swimmer?"

Ben was; I knew that from his file. "He's from California, isn't he?" I said, like that was an answer.

Then I felt a wave of panic when I saw Ben's head bobbing up and down. He was being pushed farther into the Pacific.

"But it doesn't matter if he's a super swimmer or not," I said. "If he doesn't know *not* to fight the current, he'll die from fatigue soon."

I felt my heart freeze inside my chest. Sure, I hated the guy, but not that much.

And no one was helping him.

I didn't hesitate any longer. I kicked off my shoes as I ran on the sand. Pulled my skateboard off my backpack and threw it aside.

And I dove into the water to save Ben.

20

FRIDAY, 1:51 P.M.

ON THE UPSIDE, THE UNDERCURRENT was doing a great job of pushing me toward Ben. I passed Savannah and the camera guy, who was trying to save his equipment as the boat sank.

Savannah reached to stop me. "Don't! You'll drown out there!"

"I'll be fine." I tried to look confident and heroic as I swam away, but my breaststroke was pretty rusty. I was still a few hundred yards away from Ben, and I already felt the cold water stiffening my muscles. Thankfully, I had Henry's bubbly backpack to keep me afloat.

"Come back!" someone called from the beach. I was pretty sure it was Kate. She seemed like the only one with a heart on that set, I swear.

But I felt the current help me along and push me farther from the beach. Just a few minutes and I would reach Ben. If only he stopped trying to swim to shore.

"Ben!" I called, hoping no one on shore heard me, since he was supposed to be me and all. "Don't swim! Just float."

He looked confused, but stopped swimming.

"Wait for me!" I called. I felt my backpack bob in the water, and hoped it would do some Henry magic. We really, *really* needed it. The farther away from the shore I swam, the colder the water got.

"What are you doing?" Ben said, floating in the water.

"Saving you, dude." I couldn't believe it myself. I was close enough to see his pale skin and blue lips now. Ben was hurting. "You're fighting the current," I said, keeping myself afloat a dozen feet away. "Doing that, you'll only get farther from shore—didn't they teach you this in junior secret agent boot camp?"

Ben shook his head. His tough agent attitude had washed away with the current.

I passed him my backpack. "Here. It floats, see?"

Ben grabbed it, and his arms relaxed a little. "Don't you need something to help keep yourself afloat?" His jaws chattered.

"I'm fine," I lied. My legs were already sore. "Just follow my lead, okay?"

Ben nodded. I held onto one of the backpack straps and swam parallel to the shore. "How are we getting back this way?" Ben said behind me.

"We need to swim around the current—parallel to the

shore. If you fight the riptide, it'll only push you farther out into the ocean. You gotta outsmart the current. It'll take a little while, but we'll get there."

"Makes no sense," Ben said through chattering teeth.

"You're going to argue with me, really?" I glanced back, and saw a miserable twelve-year-old kid. "Just trust me for once."

We swam—or mostly I swam, since Ben was pretty much done—for a long while, until I didn't feel the current tug at my arms and legs anymore. Then we swam to shore and crawled onto the sand.

We both collapsed on our backs.

Ben wheezed. "You said . . . you couldn't . . . swim." He coughed. "You lied."

"I saved you." I spit some salt water in the sand. "So just drop it, okay?"

Ben looked too tired to argue. After he caught his breath, he said, "This current . . . would the movie crew have known about it?"

I stretched out my arms and legs. "Maybe. Why?"

Ben sat up, and rubbed his arms. "The location where Savannah and I were . . . someone told us to go out there."

"Really?" I sat up too. "Who, Nigel Floyd?"

Ben shook his head. "The camera guy. But someone was telling him to put us there, over his headset. And it wasn't Floyd. He was just yelling his directions from the beach."

"Nice."

"Someone put us in that current. On purpose." Ben shook the sand from his hair.

"I know it's Ethan Melais," I said. "He's trying to kill me."

21

FRIDAY, 2:33 P.M.

"ETHAN MELAIS WANTS YOU DEAD?" Ben looked at me in disbelief. "But why? You're just some kid."

"You may not like that I'm on this mission, but I'm a secret agent. And that makes me a target. Melais knows I'm onto him. And he's afraid I'll uncover his identity and get the Dangerous Double."

"Maybe he's after *me* instead," Ben argued. "Clearly I'm the bigger threat, with my junior secret agent training."

"Ha!" I forced myself not to take the bait and get caught in some useless Ben argument. "The real question is: Who on the set is Ethan Melais?" I could see some people walking toward us from far away on the beach—movie crew, making sure we were still alive.

Except that one of them wanted me dead.

I felt a big chill, and it wasn't just because I was soaking wet. Maybe I seem like a tough twelve-year-old, but this was a little much, even for a fake junior secret agent.

"The lead cameraman, John," Ben said. "Even if someone did talk into his headset, he put us out in the water. We should do a background on him ASAP."

"And Kurt, the costume designer." I told Ben about the car, and the clothes hanger. I didn't share my break-in at the costume trailer; a guy needed to keep some of his secrets, right? "Floyd's assistant director, Larry, is acting suspicious, too."

"I do not think he likes me," Ben said, shivering.

I was about to tell Ben there were a lot of people who didn't like him, but that seemed a little cruel, since his lips were a dark blue and he looked like he might go into shock or something.

"We still don't have the Dangerous Double secured." Ben was looking frustrated. "This mission is a mess. I'm tired of being bait."

For once, I agreed with Ben. "It's getting too dangerous. We need to flush out the bad guy," I said. "Figure out which one of our suspects is Ethan Melais."

The crew was approaching now, and they seemed relieved that we were okay. Then some people started to look annoyed.

"This is really going to slow down the shooting, Nigel," Larry said in a whiny voice. "And the one kid looks positively blue." He pointed at Ben's face.

"We could work with that," someone said behind Larry. "With some camera filters and good lighting, you can make anyone look good."

Floyd's phone rang. He silenced it without checking who was calling. "Wrap it for the day. We'll use what we have." And he walked away.

Larry looked flabbergasted. "*We'll use what we have?*" he muttered.

"What happened to Floyd, man?" This was Kurt, the costume designer. He chewed his gum, shaking his head like he was disappointed.

"All right, enough for the day." Larry waved his hand, just like Floyd had a minute ago. "This was simply an accident; no need to blow things out of proportion. We'll see you all bright and early tomorrow." He turned to chief cameraman John and told him to send the rushes to the studio. I guessed that was the footage they'd shot that day.

"Sure thing," John said. "I guess it's just a run of bad luck: first that car crash, now this accident in the water . . ."

"Better luck tomorrow," Larry said before he turned and walked away.

The crew started to walk back to the set. No one even cared that Ben and I were basically look-alike icicles, and that we'd almost drowned out there. Where were the warm blankets, the hugs, and the offers of chicken soup?

Ben shook out his wet hair and handed me my backpack. He hesitated before saying, "Tell your friend Henry that he saved my life today." He looked me in the eye. "And I suppose you did, too. Thanks."

"You're welcome." This whole friend moment was making me feel uncomfortable, so I began to walk back in the direction of the trailers.

"Now how are we going to catch Ethan Melais?" Ben asked me as he caught up.

I didn't say anything, mostly because I had no idea.

"Are you not talking to me, Baker?"

"No, I'm just thinking." It was kind of hard with gung-ho Ben walking next to me. The dude was messing with my mojo, my thinking space. I liked it better when I had Henry with me. He knew how to get the ideas to flow.

"Ethan Melais thinks you know who he is," Ben mused, like that was helpful.

Then, suddenly, it kind of was. Because I could have Melais think I'm ready to make a deal. Tell him I want hush money.

Ben picked up speed.

I hurried to catch up. "So who on the set do *you* think is actually Ethan Melais?"

Ben stopped. He squinted, and crossed his arms in that annoying way he always does. "I will be following procedure. Gather intelligence first."

"Is that what your junior secret agent manual says? I'll bet it's soaked from your swim." And of course the airline boarding pass in my back pocket, the evidence I had that Kurt had been in Frankfurt, was destroyed.

"You have your way of doing things; I have mine." Ben got a little closer. "Let's see who's right, Baker."

"It's on. *Baker.*"

* * *

All this Baker talk made me realize I'd better go home, or Mom might nix this whole movie gig. I was in Los Angeles for the family reunion, after all. If I spent too much time away, I was asking for a random parent knee-jerk reaction. I called her, and then Mike, so I'd have a ride home.

After I dried off and used Kate's trailer to change into my regular clothes from my backpack, I decided to focus my attention on Kurt, also known as Ethan Melais. I'd have him meet me at Griffith Park, this place that has a view of the Hollywood Sign, at eight. What can I say—this whole movie thing made me feel like being dramatic about the showdown.

I hadn't exactly figured out the details yet on how I would catch the dude. Or how I would talk my parents into letting me leave the family-reunion weekend after spending all day on a Hollywood movie set. But not having a plan had never stopped me before.

I stuck a note on Kurt's trailer, hoping I wasn't making things a whole lot more dangerous for myself. Let's face it: Melais was ready to have me drown in the Pacific to protect his identity. Why not just take me out at Griffith Park?

I was getting seriously paranoid here. But then I remembered Willow's words: Just because you're paranoid doesn't mean someone isn't out to get you. And that reminded me: I'd need a ride to Griffith Park. I didn't want my cousin to tag along—there'd be too many questions, and the odds were good that he'd report back to Mom and Dad.

Maybe I'd just catch a cab.

I left the note, feeling on edge. So I jumped when I heard

a car horn honk. I looked up, and it was Savannah, waving out her car's window.

"Whoa," she said as I walked up. "Little jumpy, huh?"

"Just cold from the swim." I leaned on the open window. "How are you?"

"All dry, and ready to go home and have some soup." She pointed to her fluffy sweatshirt. Her hair was all messed up and still damp. Somehow she looked even prettier than when she was all primped for the movies.

Savannah had a car.

And I needed a ride.

"Actually, maybe you can do me a favor?" I felt a little weird asking her, but told myself it was for a good cause. The Pandora mission. Lives were at stake here—including hers. "Can you pick me up for a drive this evening?"

"Sure, why not?" Savannah leaned forward. "Where are we going?"

"I'll tell you tonight." I scribbled my aunt and uncle's address on a piece of paper and handed it to her. "It'll be cool." Only I'd have to make sure Savannah was out of the way when I met Kurt. Because Melais had tried to kill me twice already, so I had to protect Savannah. A minor hitch in my plan, but I worked best when thinking on the go anyway.

I watched Savannah's car pull away, until I could no longer read the plates.

Which reminded me of something, a detail I'd sort of forgotten about. A lead. And I knew just the person to help me out.

22

FRIDAY, 4:05 P.M.

"I HOPE YOU'RE READY FOR THE FAMILY, man." Mike gave me a crooked smile in the rearview mirror, just as we pulled into his parents' street. He and Willow had picked me up and then spent most of the way arguing about whether Chaplin had made better films than Buster Keaton. This whole movie business was wearing me out.

I didn't need to see the rest of family to know that they were here. There was Aunt Linda's truck with the silver trailer, parked at the street. I knew she had all her airbrushing equipment in there to repaint the car, because she brought it every year. My uncle Joe was down from San Francisco in his vintage Thunderbird, which he'd parked on the lawn, and my cousin Angela had left her classic Volkswagen Beetle in front of a fire hydrant.

"It's not a Baker reunion without someone parking in a tow-away zone," I joked, making my cousin snicker.

He parked his car up the road—in a legal spot—and we all walked toward the house.

"You might want to steer clear of your mom," Mike whispered before we went inside. "That whole potato-salad fiasco is making her loco, dude."

"*Macaroni* salad," I said, correcting Mike, but who knew what she was cooking up by now? Mom could get majorly stressed over this barbecue, and I really needed to focus on the mission.

"Linc, thank goodness you're here," my dad said, hurrying over the minute I closed the front door. "Your mom is on her fourth batch of macaroni salad."

"Uh-oh."

"I can't take any more onion smell, buddy." He put his arm around my shoulder, and I knew there was something he wanted from me. "Can you talk some sense into her?"

"Sure." I remembered my meeting with Melais that night. "Long as you cover for me tonight. I have a meeting with the movie people."

Dad hesitated. "You've been gone all day as it is."

I thought of Melais, and how I was sure I'd catch him tonight. "This is it, I promise."

"Okay." He pushed me toward the kitchen.

I should've asked for money or something. Or a trip to Disneyland. The onion smell was epic. I blinked. There were bowls everywhere, cutting boards with onion and celery on them—the kitchen was like a macaroni-salad war zone. "Mom?"

She looked up and smiled. Then she shoved a ladle in my face. "Taste it."

I tried a bite and spit it out. "What's in there—some weird pepper?"

"Paprika." Mom looked like she was about to cry. "It's supposed to add a unique element." She picked up this small cookbook and dropped it on the counter. "It's useless."

"Why don't you stop?"

"The barbecue is on Sunday, and I can't even get a decent salad together."

"Maybe you need a break." From the kitchen window, I saw a car drive by.

It was blue!

"I'll help you tomorrow, okay, Mom?" I rushed outside, to see what kind of car it was.

Could it be that lady who'd been following me? What if she was working with Melais?

But Aunt Linda's trailer was blocking the view. By the time I made it down the driveway, the car was gone.

And then I heard voices behind me. "It's Linc!" That was Uncle Joe. I was about to be sucked into Baker family-reunion hugs. The mission would have to wait.

A good hour later, I had a full stomach after three hot dogs off the grill and extra baked beans. I talked to all the Bakers—Mom even made an appearance, leaving the macaroni salad alone for now.

Dad showed me the rusty Town Car, looking proud. "She's got all her parts hooked up," he said, showing me the engine under the hood. The insides looked polished and shiny, like a brand-new car.

"Nice," I said. "Did you start it yet?" I knew from previous Baker reunions that a nice-looking motor didn't mean you could actually drive the car.

Dad had a worried look. "Tomorrow." He closed the hood, and we both stood there staring at the rusty exterior.

"It still looks like a lost cause."

Dad nodded. "I have faith." That's what Stark had said about my secret agent skills, but the verdict was still out on that—just like this clunker of a car.

"Where's Grandpa?" I asked as Dad closed up the garage.

He pointed toward the house. "Up in his room, watching *Cops*. You know how he hates these things."

Grandpa is more of a solitary guy. Even though this was a reunion of his kids and grandkids, it was too much talking and not enough crime solving for him. "I'll bring him a hot dog and a Dr Pepper," I said, and made my way upstairs.

Grandpa was sitting on a wicker chair, looking uncomfortable. He gave me a nod when I passed him his plate. "Thanks, kid. I was beginning to think they'd let me starve up here."

"You can come downstairs, you know." I sat on the bed.

Grandpa made a grumbling noise. "Did your mother kill anyone with her pasta salad yet?"

"Getting there."

He smiled and took a bite of his hot dog.

"Can I ask you something?" I was trying to think how to get Grandpa's help without tipping him off.

"That's already a question, but go ahead, Linc."

"This morning, when that lady came to pick me up . . ."

"The government agent," Grandpa said. He smiled when he saw my shocked expression. "You didn't think I caught that, did you? But I remembered her, from last month. When you had your Presidents Club trip to Washington, DC. She picked you up at the airport—Agent Stark. The one with the sensible shoes, FBI, CIA, NSA, some such."

I swallowed. I had no slick lie, no Linc Baker fib to get me out this time.

"Don't worry. Your secret's safe with me." Grandpa took another bite of hot dog, giving me time to get myself together.

"I was actually wondering if you could help me. Remember how you thought you saw another car?" I asked, still feeling pretty stressed out.

"And you didn't believe me."

"I do now. Remember that license plate?"

Grandpa nodded as he swallowed. He took a sip of Dr Pepper. "Sure."

I leaned forward. "Did you write it down?"

Grandpa ate his last bite of hot dog, and took his time chewing. Then he took a long swig of soda. "Hard to say, you know."

"Grandpa."

He smiled and pulled out his notebook. "7TRZ211."

I had my stalker lady.

23

FRIDAY, 7:15 P.M.

I CALLED HENRY TO HAVE HIM RUN THE stalker lady's plates, knowing Stark and Black were busy moving those Dangerous Doubles from the Pandora warehouse to safety. No sense bugging them with my hunch about this car. I told Grandpa about my meeting and I headed out.

Savannah showed up at seven fifteen on the dot. Because there was nowhere to park, her driver picked me up at the end of the road.

"So where are we going, exactly?" she asked once I buckled in.

This was the part I wasn't really sure about. Sure, I could lie to Savannah and pretend I just wanted a tour of LA or something.

Or I could do the right thing, and be honest. And I felt like I owed her the truth—plus, I was pretty sure that as an actress, she could spot a liar.

So I decided to come clean. And once I got started, I was like an avalanche of information: I told her about Pandora, Ben, and how I was kind of the stand-by choice when it came to junior secret agents. It was like someone else was talking.

I stopped when it got to the Dangerous Double—I mean, the Chaplin hat making you invisible was too dangerous to share. And she might not believe me anyway. But I did tell Savannah about Ethan Melais being a bad dude. After almost getting hit by a car, she deserved to know.

Savannah just listened the whole time, while the driver took us from my aunt and uncle's place to the Ventura Freeway and eventually to the I-5. She didn't say a thing until I was done. "Wow," she said, letting out a big sigh.

"I know, right?" I sat back in my seat. Telling the truth made me feel like I was ten pounds lighter.

"So this is your character?" Savannah sat up in her seat.

"Huh?"

"You're method acting, right? I love it." She smiled big. "I did that once, when I was playing a homeless girl. I slept outside for the night. Not actually on the street—Dad would never let me do that—but in the backyard, you know. I didn't shower for three days. Now that is not something I hope to do again. . . ." Her voice trailed.

Savannah thought I was acting. That I was pretending to be a character to get into the role.

"This isn't some movie part," I said. "I really *am* a junior secret agent. Well, sort of. A temporary one."

"Wow, you're really good, you know that?" Savannah shook her head. "Hard to believe you've never had any formal training. You're amazing, Linc."

I was about to argue with her again, but decided against it. Why argue with a girl who'd just called me amazing?

Plus, we were now climbing the hills to get to Griffith Park, so it was time for me to start being a junior secret agent.

The driver slowed as we approached the Griffith Observatory, this planetarium I'd visited when I was six. It's a giant dome, with gardens in front. The park spanned for acres around us; the road we were on looped in front of the planetarium, and over to a parking lot where I'd told Kurt to meet me.

We asked the driver to park, and got out. It was dark, but thankfully, the observatory and the parking lot were well lit. There were lots of tourists, even though it was pretty late in the day. Cars were coming and going, people taking pictures—finding Kurt might be harder than I thought. At least the crowd might keep me safe, I figured.

"Now what?" Savannah asked me.

It was almost eight o'clock. "Now we hope he shows up."

"Why did you choose Griffith Park, anyway?" Savannah asked. We walked away from the parking lot, along the overlook, where you could see the Hollywood Sign in the hills off in the distance.

"Honestly, it's a place that has lots of people around." I

watched another couple pass—tourists, judging from the cameras. "I don't want Melais to try to . . . hurt me."

"It's eight o'clock," Savannah said after checking her watch. "So this is the part where that Ethan Melais character is supposed to show up, right?" She looked all excited. "And then he'll pay you to not tell anyone who he really is. Only you'll catch him instead. Right?"

I should have told her this wasn't a game, or method acting or whatever she called it. This was serious stuff. But it was pointless, so I played along. "Exactly. And I'll hand him over to Pandora." I pulled at the straps on my new backpack, and looked for Kurt. "But you need to hang back, okay?"

"This is really awesome," Savannah said, ignoring me. She glanced around.

"Try not to look so obvious." I was getting nervous now.

"Who should I be?" Savannah whispered. "What's my character?"

"What do you mean?" She was getting on my nerves a little by now. But then I looked at her, and saw how she was totally into this acting business. "You can be my assistant or something."

"Absolutely not." She pulled my arm. "I'm nobody's assistant, sidekick, or anything."

"Sorry. You'll be my partner."

"I like that." Savannah straightened. "Maybe I can have special skills. My character could be a strong fighter—I know a little karate."

I was about to tell her that there was no need for that,

when I thought I saw a dude with a hat. A fedora, like Kurt's. He was off in the crowd, walking toward us. But I couldn't tell if it was Kurt, because he was hidden behind a group of tourists in matching yellow shirts.

"I think that might be him, over there," I told Savannah. "Stay back, okay?"

"This is so exciting," Savannah said. "It's like a real case."

"Because it is a real case!"

"Right, of course." She gave me a wink. Normally, I would have given anything for a pretty girl like Savannah to wink at me, but I needed to chase a bad dude. No time for distractions.

We rushed past the tourists, who were just not making any moves to get out of the way. And once we got to the end of the parking lot, I lost the dude in the hat.

I stopped, and so did Savannah. We both looked back along the path to the Griffith Observatory, and around the parking lot.

"If this guy is here to meet you, why is he running away from you?" Savannah asked.

That was a good point.

"Maybe he's trying to trap me," I mused, but I knew I was plain wrong. That dude in the hat probably wasn't Kurt at all; let's face it.

I turned around, and I saw a car pull up near us. A dark-blue sedan. The headlights were blinding me a little, but I didn't need to see the driver to know who it was.

Agent Black got out on the passenger side, looking as mad

as I'd ever seen him. Something was up.

Savannah asked, "That our guy?"

"No," I said. "I mean—yes, he's here for me."

Savannah smiled. "We're junior secret agents, right? Let's have a plot twist in our story, and have us stand up against the enemy. He looks kind of old anyway. I can take him." She cracked her knuckles.

"That's a really bad idea—no!"

But before I could stop her, Savannah sprinted toward Albert Black. And I don't know how she did it, but in one swift move, she pulled Black's arm.

Yanked it behind his back like she was some TV police officer.

And smacked his face on the hood of the rental.

Then she looked up at me with a triumphant grin. "I got him!"

24

FRIDAY, 8:10 P.M.

AT THAT POINT, I TOTALLY EXPECTED Albert Black to turn green and explode like the Hulk. This was not a guy who ever got his face smashed against the hood of a car as if he were some bad dude, let alone by a kid.

So I rushed over. But Stark hopped out on the driver's side and quickly pulled Savannah back.

"Hey, hey!" Stark yelled after Savannah tried to wrestle free. "We're the good guys."

"They are," I said, out of breath from my quick sprint.

Savannah wasn't buying it. "That's what the bad guys always say!" But she stopped fighting when Stark flashed her badge.

"I'm Agent Stark. You need to stand down, Savannah."

A crowd had gathered, watching this whole scuffle, unsure what to make of it.

Agent Black adjusted his shirt, looking eerily calm, like Mom does when she's at the principal's office after I get suspended. The blow-up would occur later, I knew from experience. But right then he told the crowd to take a hike. "Nothing to see here, people."

Savannah held Stark's badge. "Wait—you mean this is real?"

"I tried to tell you," I mumbled.

Savannah returned the identification to Agent Stark, who tucked it back inside her jacket.

"Maybe you want to talk in the car," Agent Stark said, giving me an urgent stare-down. A couple of the yellow-shirted tourists were giving us suspicious glances.

"I'm not getting in anyone's car." Savannah crossed her arms.

"You weren't invited." Agent Black got back in the car and slammed the door.

Stark said, "Just Linc here—and I'll drive him home."

"It's fine," I said. It was better if Savannah left, especially after she'd made Albert Black kiss the hood of this dirty rental car. "I'll see you tomorrow, okay?"

Savannah looked concerned, but nodded. "If you're sure." She left, glancing over her shoulder before disappearing in the crowd.

With all the commotion, I only now remembered why I was here in the first place. I looked around for Kurt.

"Your suspect isn't coming," Stark said when she saw me scanning the parking lot. "Ben took the note you stuck on his trailer."

"Seriously?"

"Ben may have been trying to pull one over on you, but by taking that note before Kurt could see it, he saved your cover." Agent Stark leaned closer. "Kurt couldn't have been in Italy at the time of one of the Melais thefts. He was in San Francisco on another set."

"But I found a boarding pass to Frankfurt with his name on it!"

"Did you check the date?"

I flustered.

"Get in the car." Stark opened the passenger door.

I got in, and was surprised to see a familiar face in the backseat. "Henry?"

25

FRIDAY, 8:15 P.M.

"WHAT ARE YOU DOING HERE, HENRY?"
I sat in the backseat and closed the door.

"We brought him along," Stark said before Henry could speak. "After we caught him running some car plate for you, he told us you were meeting an Ethan Melais suspect." She put the car in gear and drove away from Griffith Park.

"The plate just led to a rental company. And then Black told me to get back to the mission," Henry said. "Sorry, dude."

I shrugged.

"I had Henry here run a quick search on this Kurt," Black said. He looked like he might be ready to do that Hulk explosion now. There was a smear of car dirt on his cheek, but I figured now might not be the time to point that out.

"You got some kind of grime on your face," Henry said next to me. Way to be helpful, dude.

Black wiped his right cheek with his sleeve.

"Other side, sir," Stark said without even looking at him.

Henry snickered. "That Savannah is strong, huh? For being less than half your size."

Black shot him a death-ray after wiping his face clean. "I've about had it with you junior agents!" he barked. "Brought you in to help with the case. That was your idea, wasn't it, Stark?"

Agent Stark shook her head as she drove toward the interstate. "Not quite, sir. I believe I pointed out to *you* that bringing children on a black-ops mission was a very bad idea. There's the danger, the complicated mission directives . . ."

"Yeah, yeah." Albert Black faced forward, like he was trying to think. And calm down, hopefully.

"What Agent Black is trying to tell you kids," Stark said while she passed a slow truck on the highway, "is that you need to be more organized. Use investigative procedure, create a suspect list." Stark glanced at me in the rearview mirror. "Like when you prepare for a test at school, maybe?"

I was about to remind her of my school record but realized that was probably not a good move, since I was in the doghouse already. I had to stay on this mission. For my family's sake, and for the city of LA, I needed to do better.

Black turned around in his seat. He didn't look angry anymore. Instead he looked . . .

Scared. And that worried me more than him exploding. "Stark and I are hustling to put the Dangerous Doubles in separate hiding places so Ethan Melais can't get to them—but we're up to our eyeballs here." He pointed at me. "I'm counting on you kids, and you're monkeying around."

I swallowed.

"Where's Ben?" Stark asked. Traffic was light for once, but she stayed in the slow lane.

"Drying out his junior secret agent training manual so he can follow procedure," I mumbled.

"Well, at least one of you kids seems to be staying the course," Black said as he wiped his forehead.

"I was on the case!" I argued.

"But you're not doing any background checks or gathering evidence!" Black yelled. He pointed at Henry. "Use your resources."

Stark stopped at a red light. She turned to Black. "I think he gets it."

Black grumbled. "I hope so. Pandora is on the line here—all of the Dangerous Doubles are at risk. If those powers end up in the wrong hands . . ." He turned forward again.

"The light's green," Henry chimed in next to me.

Stark stepped on the gas.

We drove in silence the rest of the way. The longer we drove, the worse I felt.

Stark pulled over a block away from my aunt and uncle's place. I waved good-bye to Henry and got out of the car. Stark just gave me a cool nod, and Black didn't even look at me. This was worse than Mom's silent treatment after I got a bad grade.

The night air felt good, so I took my time walking back to the Baker reunion. The conversation was still bouncing around inside my head. Black was right: I had to step it up if I wanted to be a junior secret agent. I had to prove to everyone that I could be more than just the troublemaker, more than the kid who ended up with appetizers on his pants.

I was determined to catch Ethan Melais.

And to expose the bad guy, I had to do something I never thought I would.

I had to be like Ben.

26

FRIDAY, 9:15 P.M.

I MADE IT TO MY AUNT AND UNCLE'S place at nine fifteen, exhausted and frustrated from my crazy day in Hollywood. I hoped the California breeze had blown the stink of failure off me before I faced the family. Even though they didn't know it, I was flunking out as a junior secret agent. And it could cost the Bakers their lives.

The aunts and uncles were all in the backyard, sitting by the fire pit with their drinks. I waved hello and scrammed before they could ask me about the movie or want me to make s'mores or something. I needed time to think.

Which was a no-go, because Grandpa was waiting for me in the bedroom. He was watching some History Channel show on mobsters or something but turned off the set when

I came in. And Grandpa never turns off the TV. Not even for dessert.

"How was your meeting?"

I sank down on my crummy foldaway bed, tossing my backpack in the corner. "Terrible. Worse than that."

He nodded, like he knew exactly what I was talking about. "The Agency makes things complicated." He was talking about the CIA, of course.

"No kidding." I tried to lie down, but thought better of it when I felt the springs in my back. "What would you do if you were looking for someone, but they were . . . hiding?"

"In a hiding place or incognito?"

"Incog—what?"

"In disguise."

"Definitely that one, in disguise. This dude called Ethan Melais is right under my nose, but I just can't spot him."

Grandpa scooted to the edge of his bed. "You need a system—a way to track your evidence. Record what you have on paper."

"Procedures. Like a case file," I said, remembering Albert Black's scolding in the car earlier, and those blue folders with top secret stamps that Pandora kept.

"Exactly."

"That sounds like a lot of hassle," I complained. "Like homework." And I really can't stand homework.

Grandpa shrugged. "You want to catch this hoodlum or not?"

I thought of Ethan Melais and the Dangerous Double,

and how if he made it into the conference and sold the drone-system prototype to those terrorists, I'd lose my car-loving family. "Yeah, I want to catch him."

"Then you gotta do the work." Grandpa flipped the pages of his notebook and handed it to me.

Procedures. Like in Ben's junior secret agent manual. To beat him, I had to be like him. So I wrote down *Ethan Melais*. And *male, skinny*. But that was all I could come up with. I mean, the guy could be anybody, right?

I stared at that page until eventually I fell asleep. And I dreamed of the Hollywood Sign. The letters came to life and went running after me. I was at Griffith Park, and I tried to get away. But I was frozen.

27

PLACE: AN UNCOMFORTABLE FOLDAWAY BED

TIME: SATURDAY, 7:19 A.M.

STATUS: GRUMPY

I WOKE UP THE NEXT MORNING FEELING kind of groggy and tired. That stupid dream had made it even worse. Hollywood was trying to kill me, even in my sleep—and Ethan Melais was doing a bang-up job in real life. I had less than fifty hours left until the drone-prototype reveal on Monday, and I was no closer to finding Melais or the Dangerous Double. So I wasn't really feeling like getting up.

Of course Grandpa didn't mind helping me there. Once he got out of the shower, he rudely pulled the covers off the bed.

"Hey, Grandpa!" I tried to tug at the corner of my

blanket, but it was out of reach.

"Time to get up, kid." Grandpa started making his bed, leaving me in a cloud of his cologne.

So I took a shower, letting the hot water jump-start my brain. As hard as it was to find Ethan Melais and the Dangerous Double, I only had to think of my family to remember why I was on the case.

Before I left, I grabbed my backpack. Including a notebook this time. I had no idea how I was going to create a case file, but I would get some help with that.

On my way out the door, I passed the freshly sanded Town Car. Aunt Linda would be airbrushing the body today, I knew from all the other car overhauls at Baker reunions. But unless Dad got the thing to start, it would just be a pretty lawn decoration.

Dad was hunched over the engine and didn't even look up when I called, "Hey, Dad. Where'd everyone go?"

Dad groaned. "I probably scared them off." That was very un-Dad-like. He's the nicest guy you could ever meet.

"Uh-oh." I adjusted my backpack and heard the compass ding against the rusty metal of the old Town Car.

"Can't figure out why she won't start." Dad stepped back from the engine and took off his glasses. He wiped the lenses on his shirt.

I wanted to stick around and help, but I had to go. If I didn't find this Melais and the Dangerous Double, my family wouldn't be around to celebrate the next reunion. "Can't anyone give you a hand?"

"The engine is my game, Linc, you know that. Maybe it's the water pump," Dad muttered. He put on his glasses and disappeared under the hood.

"Good luck with it, Dad. I gotta go," I said.

"Wait," he said, and looked up. "How long will you be gone for?"

"I put the call sheet on the fridge." And I took off before he could ask any more questions.

Stark was waiting for me at the end of the block. "Morning," she said once I got in. She waited for me to put on my seat belt before driving away. Her expression was grim as she sipped from a Styrofoam cup.

So I didn't say anything. With adults, you have to know when to let them get their coffee fix.

"Do you have a plan?" Stark finally asked once we got onto the highway.

"I'm working on a profile."

Stark lingered in the slow lane, seeming superstressed.

"I just need to narrow my suspect list. There are about a hundred dudes left on the set. . . ." I was beginning to depress myself.

"Henry is having the Melais business card checked for prints." Stark gulped her coffee. "This case is a nightmare. Black and I have only secured half of the Dangerous Doubles, so we can't help you kids. The weapon reveal is in two days. We're running out of time!"

I didn't know what to say to that. We drove in silence for a while, and I felt kind of nervous. What if we couldn't complete this mission? What if Melais made it to the reveal on Monday and stole the drone? We had less than forty-eight hours left.

This was bad.

We'd arrived a block or so away from the Santa Monica Pier, and I unbuckled my seat belt.

Agent Stark looked me in the eye. "Honestly, you and Ben are our best shot at uncovering Ethan Melais's identity, since you're right here on the set. Black and I could never have the access you do. We need that Dangerous Double."

No pressure or anything.

I got out and walked the block to the pier, passing colorful storefronts. The street was so packed with tourists I didn't even bother riding my skateboard. I reached Ocean, the avenue that runs along the beach, and crossed the bike path. The Santa Monica Pier was up ahead. I saw that the north parking lot had a bunch of trailers parked on it.

But all the crew and cast were gathered near the entrance to the pier, so that's where I headed. I could hear Floyd yelling from a few dozen yards away.

"This is rubbish!" He crumpled up a piece of paper and threw it at Larry's chest.

Larry calmly bent down to pick it up. He said something to Floyd that I couldn't hear from a distance.

"I don't care if it's a legal document!" Floyd hollered, practically spitting in Larry's face. Floyd needed to lay off the caffeine, or play some video games to relax a little. The guy looked like he was going to wring Larry's neck.

I couldn't see Larry's face, but I did spot Savannah. She gave me a smile and a little wave, which made me walk twice as fast.

"Everyone, take fifteen." Floyd waved his hand. "Heck, take an hour for all I care!" he yelled over his shoulder as he stormed off toward the trailers.

He pushed John, the chief camera guy, out of the way.

John gave Floyd a dark look. "You know, there are other people on the set. People who deserve respect."

But Floyd was too far away to hear him.

"What happened?" I asked Savannah. Around us, crew members scattered, looking defeated and grumpy.

Savannah got closer. She was wearing her hair in a braid this time. "I guess Floyd got a court order. Something to do with money."

"He's broke, right?" And he was taking it out on Larry, who was my number two suspect for Ethan Melais. If Larry sold that drone-system prototype, he could bail Floyd out. Or better still: He'd never have to work for Floyd again.

Savannah said, "This place is getting crazy. It's starting to feel like an Alan Smithee project."

Huh?

When she saw my confused expression, Savannah explained, "Alan Smithee is a name directors use if they don't want their own associated with a movie."

"Like putting someone else's name on your English paper."

"Exactly." Savannah looked troubled. "Nigel is acting like

he doesn't care about this movie."

"So now what do we do?" I asked.

Savannah exhaled. "We wait." She stepped closer, and glanced around. "How is your case coming along?"

I hesitated. How much could I tell her? "It's stalled, like an old car." No point lying. I spotted the Crepes-to-Go truck and pulled Savannah along.

"Where are we going?"

"Come on. I want you to meet a friend of mine. He'll help me fix this case."

28

SATURDAY, 9:35 A.M.

"I HEARD ABOUT THIS PLACE," SAVANNAH said as we got closer to the food truck. "Apparently these crepes are legendary—the chefs are from France."

I laughed. "They've visited, yeah," I said, thinking of my first mission, in Paris.

Of course the crepe stand was closed, but the door was open. I peeked inside and was greeted by a cranky Albert Black.

"What are you doing here, kid?" He stood in the kitchen. Stark was hunched over some papers on the counter. She looked very tired.

Henry peeked from around the banquette corner. He grinned, looking relieved to see me.

"Can I borrow Henry for a minute?" I asked.

"Why?"

"I'm using my resources, like you said."

Henry jumped up.

Black sighed and said, "Go, but don't take too long."

Henry rushed to join me, and he let out a groan once he closed the door.

"High stress in there, huh?" I said, thumbing at the Crepes-to-Go truck.

Henry nodded, and straightened when he spotted my sidekick—or partner, as she liked to be called.

"Hi, I'm Savannah." She extended her hand and smiled.

Henry looked like he was about to faint. He wiped his hand on his pants before shaking hers. "I'm Henry. You were on that TV show, um, *You Only Live Once*."

Savannah made a face. "Not the best listing on my résumé, but yes."

Henry just looked at her with his mouth gaping.

"Dude, we need your brainpower." I put my arm around his shoulders and directed him to a deserted picnic bench. I sat down and pulled out my notebook. "I need your help narrowing the pool of Ethan Melais suspects."

Savannah and Henry sat down. Henry looked a bit more relaxed now that he had something to focus his brilliant brain on.

"Tell me what they teach you in junior secret agent boot camp." I had missed that particular stint of misery, but Henry hadn't. "I need to follow some sort of procedure, or I'll never catch Melais."

Henry snickered. "You know, you sound like Ben."

"Don't remind me." I clicked my pen.

"Okay," Henry said, getting more serious. "You have to start with a list of Melais's attributes. I can just get the file and save you some time there."

Henry went inside the trailer and came out with the file. "Height—average. That's not helpful. Weight—slender."

"I already have that," I said, waving my notebook. "It describes a few dozen guys on the crew.

"I get what you're doing," Savannah said. "You're creating a character profile."

"You're aware this isn't pretend, right?" I said. "We're not method acting here or whatever."

She waved my comments away. "I know *that*. But you're not sure who this guy is, right? So you have to figure it out with the information you have—I do the same thing when I work on a character."

"That makes sense," Henry said. "We're building a profile, only a criminal one. So let's describe him. He's a master thief. Dresses like a gentleman. Knows how to sneak in and out of places without getting caught, but then likes to rub people's noses in it by leaving a business card. Does that about cover it?"

I nodded, still scribbling in my notebook.

"He's frustrated," Savannah said. She stared off into the distance. "This character is someone who wants more credit for what he does—that's what the business card is all about."

"'Look at me—I'm Ethan Melais,'" I mumbled as I wrote

it in my notebook. I felt energized. We were getting somewhere. I could feel it.

"Maybe this guy is quiet, but underappreciated," Savannah mused.

"The cameraman!" I said. I closed my notebook and stuffed it into my backpack. "John was all mad at Floyd, remember? He was talking about deserving respect. That makes sense. He put Ben out in the current." Turns out Ben was right after all. It was a good thing he wasn't here, or he'd rub it in. Where was my annoying double anyway?

Savannah said, "John might still be at the pier."

"Let's catch him!" Henry jumped up.

Savannah did too.

"You guys know this dude is dangerous, right?" I asked.

They each nodded, which I took as an I-don't-care. So we rushed away from the trailers.

"We probably shouldn't be running," I said. We slowed.

But then I saw Ben walking up on the Santa Monica Pier. What if he beat me to the punch?

No way. I clenched my teeth.

And ran.

29

SATURDAY, 10:25 A.M.

THE SANTA MONICA PIER HAD BEEN BAR-ricaded for our movie, just like the Chinese Theatre. There were a couple of security guys hanging around. I just waved at them and ran past.

No one was going to slow me down. Not even Ben Green.

Lucky for me, I saw John, the chief camera guy, up ahead near the Looff Hippodrome. It's this historical building with an old-fashioned carousel inside. My aunt Jenny took me there once when I was little. The building has many entryways, each arched—my bad dude John was standing near one of them.

He was busy studying papers on a clipboard—probably more plans to kill me, since he was actually Ethan Melais. I was just fifty yards away from him. I didn't know exactly how I was going to bring in my suspect. There was probably some sort of tactic they taught junior secret agents.

But it didn't matter what I had planned. Because John turned and disappeared inside the Hippodrome.

It took me another ten seconds to reach the building and get inside. I heard the music—someone had turned on the carousel!

The wood of the deserted carousel creaked as it slowly picked up speed. The old-fashioned horses moved up and down, making it hard to spot my bad guy. I decided to jump onto the carousel. What better way to close in on him without actually having to run, right?

I got on, grabbing a white horse with a purple saddle to steady myself. This thing moved faster than I'd expected. I scanned the area and caught a glimpse of someone disappearing around the center.

There was another person on the carousel! Probably John. I reached behind me for my backpack. All I had to do was grab my bad dude by the wrist and use the Instacuff to attach him to the carousel.

It was a great plan.

I put my backpack back on and clutched the two straps that made up the Instacuff. Confident I could take the guy down, I walked around the moving horses, but it was harder than you'd think, with the carousel spinning at the same time. And I couldn't see the bad dude anymore.

I hurried to the edge of the carousel so I could avoid the

horses and go faster. I rushed, until I was just feet away from John, my bad dude.

I was about to take my last few steps to grab my bad dude. Only I felt a strong jerk at my backpack.

I was stuck on something! It yanked me off the carousel.

I fell back, and realized who'd pulled me off.

Ben Green.

"What are you doing?" I moved away and sat on the floor.

"Saving you from making a fool of yourself!" Ben spat at me. He pushed me aside and stood up. "As usual."

I sat up, watching John disappear. He didn't even look back. "You just let my prime suspect escape!"

Savannah and Henry had caught up by now and were watching me be humiliated by Ben.

I stood up and brushed the dirt off my pants. I tucked the Instacuff inside my pocket. "John was my best lead. You know, he put you at the far end of the water, into that strong current."

"No, he didn't." Ben closed his eyes and took a breath, like he was controlling his anger.

I was ready to punch his lights out. "You told me that yourself!"

"Floyd ordered it, or at least John thinks he did. Maybe his assistant director is calling the shots—heck, I don't know." Ben stepped closer. "John can't be Ethan Melais," he whispered, so Henry and Savannah couldn't hear.

"What did you say?" Henry called. Savannah looked confused.

"He's not our bad guy." I caught Ben's peeved expression. I added, "Savannah already knows about the case. Now wait—why not?"

Ben still kept an eye on Savannah. "John doesn't have a passport. No way to travel, so . . ."

"He can't be Ethan Melais," I mumbled, feeling the defeat. It was a good thing I hadn't tried to Instacuff the guy.

"John is heading back to the set. You need to leave him alone, Baker." Ben straightened his shirt. I noticed he was wearing his usual clothes—a black T-shirt, black cargo pants, and black boots. I guess the airline had found his suitcase. Ben said, "We can't talk about the case. There are civilians here. You may be comfortable playing this one loose and easy, but I'm not. I'm going by the book."

"How very predictable," I said.

Ben turned and walked toward the exit. "You need to just stay out of my way," he called over his shoulder.

For a split second I was ready to run after him, and tell him what was what. But then I realized: My suspect list for Ethan Melais had just dwindled down to two guys. The ones who controlled the set.

Nigel Floyd and his assistant director, Larry.

30

SATURDAY, 11:00 A.M.

I WAS FEELING PRETTY SMUG AS I walked away from the Santa Monica Pier. Even though Ben had just tackled me, things were looking up: I had narrowed my list to two suspects, and I didn't even need to update my case file or anything. It was like getting an A on a test without even studying.

Savannah and Henry were walking back to the trailers with me. I scanned the pier for Floyd and Larry, but neither guy was around. Not even past the roadblocks.

"So now what?" Savannah asked me.

I stopped. "I don't know." Normally, I like to just fly by the seat of my pants. But this time, I wanted to have some sort of tactical plan, like a real secret agent. And I worried about what Melais had planned for me next.

Savannah checked her watch. "Well, I'd better check with Kate before Nigel decides he's ready to shoot again." She huffed. "For a movie set, there's very little moviemaking going on."

We watched her walk away. And I kind of got to thinking after what she said about the moviemaking stuff. "You think that Floyd is a stronger suspect?"

"Because he's not filming much?" Henry pondered that thought. "I guess." He shrugged. "I'm the tech guy. I didn't pay attention that much when they covered field-agent procedures."

I saw the lighting and camera crew approach. "Let's keep walking."

"So now what—are we going to bust them both?" Henry asked, all excited.

"We need proof," I said. We'd stopped in front of the Crepes-To-Go trailer. "Can you find out if either Floyd or Larry was in Frankfurt when Ethan Melais was there?" I asked Henry.

Henry grinned. "Leave it to me." He opened the trailer door, and I was about to follow him inside when a voice bellowed behind me.

"We're shooting in ten, people!"

I felt my stomach twist, like when you miss the second bell at school. Only this was a lot worse. They were shooting another scene. And the bad dude, whether it was Floyd or Larry, was still out there. Wanting me dead.

"That means you, Linc Baker!"

I turned around and came face-to-face with Larry, who gave me the nastiest look I'd ever seen. He shoved the costume at me. Someone had obviously washed and dried it after yesterday's swim in the Pacific. "Put that on. Now."

I hurried inside the trailer and changed as fast as I could, transferring the Instacuff straps to my costume pants. I grabbed my backpack.

Before I went outside, Henry said, "I'll get right on that search."

I nodded, but my confidence disappeared like a birthday balloon in the wind. Truth was, on that movie set I was basically an easy target for the bad guy. A giant bull's-eye, a sitting duck—well, you get the idea. I had to find Ethan Melais. *Now.*

"Let's go." Larry motioned toward the Santa Monica Pier with his clipboard.

I hurried along, catching up with Savannah. The pier looked like a scene in a scary movie. It was all fogged over, making the wood planks slippery under my 1930s shoes. I wished I was able to wear my sneakers—heck, I wished I wasn't there at all.

Reluctantly, I left my backpack with some of the crew.

Floyd showed up, looking distracted. And worried. Maybe he knew he was about to be busted for being Ethan Melais. He sat down in the director's chair. "Let's shoot, yeah?"

"Whatever you want, Nigel," Larry said. He walked over to have a conversation with John.

"They want us to ride the Ferris wheel." Savannah pointed

to it. There was a roller coaster that looped around it like a snake. The cars were like cups, with umbrellas above them, alternating red and yellow.

"Don't they have stunt people for this?" I asked.

"Floyd doesn't use those—it's more authentic," Savannah answered.

That's what I was afraid of. Looking at the Ferris wheel, I felt a tinge of dread inside my gut, but I shrugged it off. I mean, people took this ride all the time, right?

"Nigel, are you ready?" Larry asked.

Floyd looked lost in thought.

"Nigel!"

He looked up. "Yeah, sure."

Seemed like Larry was calling a lot of the shots. That put him at the top of my suspect list—if only I could go check in with Henry, see if he'd been able to link Larry or Floyd to the exact times and locations of the Ethan Melais thefts.

"You kids walk around, like you're here for the first time in your life." Floyd pointed to the Ferris wheel. "Then you'll walk over there, and we'll cut."

"That's it—we're just walking?" I felt relief wash over me like a wave.

"We'll superimpose this scene over one we're shooting next week, with David Graham." Floyd added in a mumble, "If we can get the funding to come through."

It got so quiet on the set you could hear the wind blow around us. I took it that this money issue was a biggie. And a huge motivation to want to steal those secrets at the summit, if Floyd was Melais.

"We're running out of time, Nigel," Larry said behind us, having snuck up like a ninja again.

"Let's do this thing, then." Floyd stepped back and returned to his chair. He sat down and called, "Action!"

Savannah walked, and I followed. I felt like an idiot, if you want to know the truth. How was this going to make for a good movie?

We reached the Ferris wheel and Larry hollered, "Cut! Next scene."

Savannah and I turned around. Floyd was motioning to someone behind the Ferris wheel. This guy in a blue polo shirt turned a switch on the control panel and walked to the front.

"You kids ready to get on?" he asked. The wheel made a little creaking noise as it came to a stop.

We both got on one of the yellow cars, and it was awkward for a second, since we were sitting very close to each other.

"And we're back!" Larry stood near the Ferris wheel, and stepped aside as a lady with a camera got closer. "Silence on the set. We shoot in five, four, three, two . . ."

Savannah and I rode the wheel once, and again we weren't saying any lines at all. While we were at the top, I heard Larry yell, "CUT!" We rode the rest of the way down, and the Ferris wheel was stopped just as we were reaching the ground.

"This is going to be a seriously lame movie," I said to Savannah. "Nothing happens." I saw the camera lady get into the car in front of us. "Wait—what is she doing?"

"She'll get a different angle." Savannah pointed at the camera lens, which was now pointed squarely at us. "Just act like the Hollywood kid."

I was about to ask her what that meant, when the Ferris wheel got back in motion with a jerk.

Savannah shifted in her seat. "Whoa," she muttered under her breath.

I forced myself to stay quiet as our car passed over the ground, then moved us up again. The fog floating from the Pacific seemed to get thicker. The wheel was speeding up—that wasn't in the script, was it?

We were at the top now, and I felt a wobble. Like something above us was loose.

"What's happening?" Savannah mumbled, trying not to move her lips.

"I don't know." We were descending, and definitely at a faster speed than before. "Maybe we should jump out down below." I didn't care about the movie—I just wanted off.

The camera lens wasn't pointed at us anymore. The camera lady had figured out something was wrong, too. She glanced around, looking panicked.

The Ferris wheel sped over the ground, giving us no time to jump out of the car.

Savannah whimpered next to me as we swooped up again, toward the gray sky.

This was not good.

"Hold on," I said, like that was helpful. Truth was, I had

no idea what to do. And my gadgets were inside my backpack, which was on the ground.

Suddenly the Ferris wheel came to a halt, jerking the car, making it swing back and forth.

There was a poof, like something exploded. Then a cracking noise above us, where the umbrella was attached to the wheel. In the car ahead of us, the lady dropped her camera. It shattered against the metal bars.

Savannah screamed.

I don't know why, but I grabbed her hand. I looked up, and through the foggy mist I saw our umbrella come off on one side.

Then I heard a crack.

Our car was coming loose.

I had to do something, or we'd plummet to the ground.

Savannah squeezed my hand. Her eyes scared me more than the sound of the moaning steel above us.

"Don't let go of my hand," I said.

"I won't."

The umbrella was attached by just a tiny sliver of welded steel.

I heard a crack.

And I saw the umbrella come loose. Below our feet, the car dropped.

31

SATURDAY, 12:05 P.M.

I QUICKLY GRABBED THE STEEL POST that held the umbrella. And used the crooked Ferris wheel car as leverage with my sneakers.

Savannah screamed. She gripped my waist but was dangling—I had to do something. *Quick.*

And then I remembered Henry's Instacuff! I had those two straps in my pocket from earlier.

Thank you, Henry.

"I'm slipping!" Savannah's voice was so full of panic my heart almost stopped.

Using one hand, I reached behind me and strapped her wrists so she was now hugging me, with her hands cuffed at my back, all while I gripped the umbrella post with my other hand. I had to push my feet hard against the Ferris wheel car to keep us both from falling.

Someone managed to get the wheel moving again. There was a jerking motion, but I held on.

Savannah's face was wet with tears—and to be honest, I kind of felt like crying myself. I cursed Ben as I struggled to keep my grip on the metal bar. If only he was a better actor, he would be dangling off this stupid Ferris wheel right now.

Once we reached the ground, the camera lady was saved from her broken car. The whole crew clapped and hooted. Someone brought me my backpack, and I used a set of magnets to unhook a dazed Savannah. We were both trembling, and I felt dizzy.

But I did catch a glimpse of Larry, who looked seriously angry. Maybe because his plan to kill me had failed.

Floyd was gone.

My legs were shaking as I walked away from the Ferris wheel. Savannah was still clinging to my arm.

"Are you okay?" I looked over and saw that she was still crying. But her tears were quiet, angry tears.

"Fine." Savannah squeezed my hand and bit her lip. "Actually, I'm not fine at all." She wiped the tears from her face. "That's it! I quit—I don't care if this is a Nigel Floyd film. Someone's been trying to kill us on every set. I'm calling my mom!"

Most of the crew was inspecting the Ferris wheel, so thankfully, they paid no attention to Savannah's outburst.

But I saw that Larry was keeping an eye on us.

Savannah didn't care. "I'm out." She turned to Larry. "You can tell Floyd that."

Larry didn't even blink.

Savannah looked at me. "I'll see you at the Hollywood Bowl tribute to the Oscars tonight." She let go of my hand and stalked away.

Larry looked at me. "And you—are you scared too?"

Thinking of my family's safety, I smiled. "Nope. You're stuck with me." I wasn't going anywhere—I was right on Ethan Melais's tail, I could feel it.

Larry squinted. "We'll have to find a body double for Savannah—this will take some serious editing," he said, mostly to himself. Then to me: "Go freshen up. We're back in twenty."

I walked away, feeling like I'd won. But I was also hoping no one saw how my legs were shaking. And I still didn't know: Was Floyd Ethan Melais, or was Larry?

"No way! Duuuude . . ." Henry listened to my story in the crepe truck. His jaw kept dropping lower and lower the further I got into it.

"So thank you for that Instacuff," I said in the end. "Without them, Savannah and I would have fallen right off that Ferris wheel." I shivered at the thought.

Agent Stark had just gotten off the phone, and she was listening to the story, too. "This case is getting out of hand. We have to find Ethan Melais, *now*." She sat down with us.

"Black and I are almost done with securing the Dangerous Doubles from the warehouse. So we can help you soon. But Linc—you and Ben are still our best shot at finding Melais, since you have full access to the set."

"I'm trying, believe me," I said, feeling like a failure.

Stark turned to Henry. "Are you getting anywhere?"

Henry shook his head. "I first tried to track that business card, see if I could link the paper or design to a manufacturer. But that went nowhere—too common. No prints, so that was a dead end." He sighed. "Now I'm trying to track the crew's travel records. I thought it would be easy, but none of our suspects shows up on passenger manifests."

"They probably chartered a flight," Stark mused.

"Of course! I'll search for that." Henry turned back to his laptop.

Agent Stark nodded. "We all have to get back to work. It's already Saturday, and we still don't have Ethan Melais or the Dangerous Double."

"Where's Albert Black?" I asked.

Stark thumbed to the driver's compartment of the food truck, looking worried. "He's busy calling his contacts, relocating the last of the Dangerous Doubles. Pandora is in serious jeopardy with the Chaplin hat out there unsecured." Suddenly she seemed annoyed. "Where's Ben?"

"I don't know," I said, like I didn't care. But where was the dude, anyway? I'd bet he'd been studying that stupid junior secret agent manual while I was dangling off a Ferris wheel.

Stark turned away and tried to call Ben. No answer.

Someone knocked on the door, and Stark opened, hollering, "We're out of batter, so go away!" She groaned after closing the door.

Henry looked up from his laptop. "This is impossible. How am I going to get passenger lists for all these chartered flights?"

"Maybe we're looking at this all wrong," I said, thinking out loud. "Larry and Floyd wouldn't just take a plane, right?"

"I don't know what you're getting at," Stark said, looking confused.

But Henry did. He grinned, pointing his finger at me. "Hotels! They would need to stay at a hotel, right?"

Stark perked up. "That's good. But which hotel . . . ?"

"A big one." I thumbed to the trailer door. "Look out there—Floyd comes with a whole gang of sidekicks. They would take up a big chunk of hotel."

Henry's fingers were flying over the laptop keys. "Give me a few minutes and I'll have that information."

Stark nodded. "I'll leave you to it. I'd better go help Albert Black contact Pandora operatives, to secure the last of the Doubles." She left us to join Black in the driver's compartment.

Just then, my phone rang. The call showed up as unavailable, but I answered anyway. "Hello?"

"You didn't call me." It was Mom. "And I didn't even see you at breakfast. You were supposed to check in at lunch, remember?"

"Sorry," I said. "I just got . . . hung up a little." This was entirely true: I had been dangling off that Ferris wheel. "How is the macaroni salad?"

"Good." Mom was mad.

"I'm really sorry I forgot to call," I said.

"Where are you shooting right now?"

Uh-oh. Mom was thinking of crashing the set. "Santa Monica. But we're changing locations, I think."

"You think?" Mom huffed. "I'm coming out there. It's about time I meet this director."

"No!" I took a breath. Henry gave me a worried look. "Let me find out where we're shooting next, okay?"

Mom was silent.

"Then you can meet the dude."

"Okay. I expect a call soon. And Linc?"

"Yeah."

"This is beginning to smell like one of your troublemaking episodes."

"It's not. Honest."

We hung up just in time, because there was a bunch of shouting near the trailer. I moved the tiny curtain over the window. Outside, people were scrambling. I saw the back of Larry's head, and I was pretty sure he was yelling about shooting in five or something.

"I have to get to the set." I felt a brick drop inside my stomach.

"No way, man." Henry glanced up from his laptop, looking all upset. "You can't go back there!"

"I have to keep the cover up." I motioned to Henry's

laptop. "Especially with you almost cracking the case."

Henry shook his head, but he knew I was right. "I did just narrow down the list of hotels," he said. "We're close."

Maybe too close. And Ethan Melais knew it.

I left the Crepes-to-Go truck, feeling like I did when I got called to the principal's office. Only a whole lot worse.

I walked toward the Santa Monica Pier, where the fog was even thicker now. Floyd sat in his director's chair, and the crew was setting up cameras around the Ferris wheel.

Larry waved me over, clipboard in hand. "Change of plans, Linc."

"Everyone!" Floyd hollered. "That footage on the Ferris wheel was brilliant—what a marvelous tribute to *Safety Last!*"

"Huh?" I said.

Larry shook his head. "It's a famous Harold Lloyd film, where he dangles off a tall building from a clock—don't you watch any movies?"

I was about to tell him I mostly watch crime shows with Grandpa and play Racing Mania Nine, but Larry raised his hand to silence me.

"I want to thank everyone for their efforts, but I have some bad news," Floyd said with a sigh. "Filming of *The Hollywood Kid* has been suspended."

"What does that mean?" I asked, though I knew very well.

"It means you're all going home," Floyd said. "We're done."

32

SATURDAY, 1:15 P.M.

AT FIRST, I WAS ACTUALLY A LITTLE relieved. If suspending the movie meant I could skip the next ride on the Ferris wheel, I saw it as a big plus.

Then I realized this would keep me from finding Melais and the Chaplin hat. This wasn't good at all.

Floyd took off, and the crew scattered, gathering equipment. Larry gave directions where needed, but then he walked back toward the trailers too.

My suspects were getting away. And there was nothing I could do to stop them.

I was just standing there on the Santa Monica Pier, when I saw Henry running toward me.

"They shut down the movie?" he asked once he reached me.

I nodded. "Out of money is the official report."

"But how are you going to get close to Ethan Melais now?" Henry asked.

"I'm not." I started walking back toward the trailers, feeling like a total failure.

"Well, maybe you don't need to be dangling off Ferris wheels anymore." Henry smiled. "I found out that Larry can't be Ethan Melais. That's why I came to find you on the set. We narrowed down the list of hotels in Frankfurt. Stark got on the phone and hit pay dirt on the first one: The crew was staying at the Wienerschnitzel Inn during one of Melais's thefts."

We got closer to the trailers. Some were already hitched to trucks, and a big bus was filling up with crew members.

Henry continued, "Just about the entire movie crew got sick. Guess they had some bad schnitzels or something." He made a face. "They ended up in the ER, and most spent a day in the hospital. Including Larry."

My heart sank. "So does that mean we're back at square one? No suspects?"

Henry shook his head and smiled. "Guess who never got sick?"

"Nigel Floyd."

"Bingo."

"So he's Ethan Melais!" I said, maybe a little loud. But the crew was too busy packing up to pay attention to me.

Henry said, "We probably need more proof than a bad schnitzel, you know."

"You're right." But at least I was down to one suspect now.

We reached the Crepes-to-Go truck and rushed inside. I had to catch up with Agent Stark before it was too late and Floyd was gone with the foggy Pacific wind. I had to save my family, save LA.

Inside, Stark had packed up the paperwork and Black was preparing to drive away.

Ben was sitting in the banquette, writing on a small notepad. He closed it when he saw me. "If it isn't the unwanted element," he said, looking smug.

Suddenly I got really mad at Ben. "Where were you?" I leaned on the banquette table.

Ben tucked the notepad in his pocket, all cool and collected. "I traced a lead. It didn't pan out."

"What lead?" A droplet of spit went flying. I was so angry my whole body trembled like there was an earthquake inside my chest. "Our suspect is out there on the set, and you left me to fend off the bad dude by myself!"

Ben blinked.

"Where were you?" I leaned closer, trapping him in the banquette seat. "You know I ended up hanging off a Ferris wheel?"

Ben tried to sit back to get away from me, but there wasn't room in the tight banquette.

I got up in his face. "Nice work, leaving me as a target."

Someone touched my shoulder. "Enough," Stark said.

I backed off. But I still felt so angry I thought I might punch the guy.

"What's this all about, Agent Green?" Stark asked, careful

to stand between me and Ben.

Ben sat up and brushed back his hair. "I broke into Larry's house to retrieve the Dangerous Double."

"And?" Stark looked optimistic.

"It wasn't there," Ben said softly.

"Enough with the bickering, kids. Sit down—I'm driving away," Black said from the driver's seat. Stark took shotgun and put on her seat belt.

Henry and I settled into the booth, opposite Ben. We had no choice.

"Where are we going?" Henry asked.

"We've made arrangements for all of Pandora's Dangerous Doubles to be relocated to top secret locations," Black said. "Right now, we're returning this truck."

"And then what?" I asked.

"We try to find Floyd, since he's our prime suspect." Stark sat down in the passenger seat. "He's taken off, and he's been known to disappear for days at a time."

"Pretty handy, if you're really Ethan Melais," I said.

"How are we going to catch him?" Henry asked. He sounded kind of panicked.

Neither Stark nor Black said anything for a few seconds. Then Stark said softly, "Our only chance may be at the drone-system reveal in Las Vegas on Monday. We'll have to hope he doesn't slip past me again."

Those were not good odds.

"But first we'll drop Linc off with his family," Stark said. "You have a reunion to get ready for, don't you?" Her voice was friendly, but the message was clear.

I was off the case.

"The reunion, yeah." I felt a tug of disappointment. And fear. What if that terrorist group got hold of the drone-system prototype and used it on LA? What if there wasn't another reunion next year?

I called Mom and told her the movie was a wrap, and that I was on my way home. She was on batch number fifteen of her macaroni salad and was all excited I would be helping her cut the vegetables.

Next to me, Ben was poring over his notebook. Henry was on his laptop, trying to compile the list of upcoming charter flights out of LA, to figure out where Floyd might be headed next. Stark and Black were talking about the case up in front.

I tuned it out. I tried to think of an argument, a reason Pandora should let me stay. But I couldn't think of one.

Ben was the real agent, and I was just a kid.

I was done being a junior secret agent. There was nothing I could do anymore.

Still, out of all of us in the truck, I had the most to lose.

33

SATURDAY, 3:00 P.M.

WE WERE STUCK IN TRAFFIC FOR ABOUT an hour, making everyone even grumpier. Black dropped me off at the end of my aunt and uncle's street. Nobody said much along the way—I'm sure we were all thinking the same thing. This case was a real stinker. Henry waved me good-bye, and Black barely waited for my sneakers to hit the pavement before punching the gas. So much for us being a team.

I was out.

At my aunt and uncle's place, the driveway was empty, and there was a sheet of heavy plastic taped along the front of the garage. That meant Aunt Linda was inside, airbrushing the Town Car. Aunt Jenny was sweeping the driveway.

"How's the movie biz, Linc?" she called when I walked up.

I shrugged. No way could I fake enthusiasm now, not

with the movie and the case pretty much out of my hands. "It's a wrap."

"That's Hollywood for you." She gave me a smile. "At least you got to miss the drama here." She told me about the Town Car, and how the engine had sort of blown up on them. Dad and Uncle Tim were out in El Segundo, on the hunt for replacement parts. "This is the worst I've seen these overhauls, Linc. I finished the bench seats, and your aunt Linda is doing the body work in there. But without an engine . . ."

"It's a failure," I said, finishing her thought. Kind of like me as a junior secret agent.

Just then, Mom came outside with two glasses of lemonade. "You're back."

I explained to her why the movie was a wrap. "I don't think I'm cut out for it." The lemonade was cold and tart. "How about your macaroni salad?"

Aunt Jenny laughed.

"What?" I could have used a laugh, honestly.

"I taught your mom how I make the best baked beans in the state," Aunt Jenny said. "By opening a can."

Mom leaned close. "I went to the grocery store. Turns out they make a killer macaroni salad in the deli department, so I pretended I made it." She grinned.

Go, Mom.

Since she was already in a good mood, I asked if I could go see Savannah perform at the Hollywood Bowl.

"This is that pretty actress—Ava Stone's daughter?" Mom smiled and gave me a wink. "She must like you a lot, to invite you to such a special event."

Aunt Jenny elbowed me with a big grin. This was getting embarrassing.

"She's just a friend. So can I go?"

Mom agreed. "Have your cousin drive you, and call me when you're on your way home."

I nodded. "Is Grandpa upstairs?"

"Of course." Mom sighed.

"See if you can get him to come down for some food, okay, Linc?" Aunt Jenny asked.

I found Grandpa doing a crossword on his bed. He tossed it aside the minute he saw me come in. "Linc! How's the hunt for criminals?"

"Not good." I sat on my uncomfortable foldaway bed and told him about my day: the Ferris wheel, Larry not being the bad guy, and Floyd wrapping up the movie—the whole story. Grandpa just nodded, and frowned at the end of it.

"So your hoodlum flew the coop, huh?" he said, shaking his head.

"I guess so."

"Something's not right," Grandpa said. "It's like a bad puzzle, where some fool came in and crammed the pieces in the wrong spot. You know your Ethan Melais fellow?"

"Uh-uh." Tired and fed up, I leaned back on the bed and stretched my legs.

Grandpa pulled out a piece of paper. "I thought the name was off. Did you know that when you scramble the letters, you come up with all kinds of other names? That thief's name is an anagram, Linc. Does 'the Alias Men' mean anything to you?"

"No," I said with a sigh.

"Or Alaine, or something—I got all kinds of possibilities here . . . ," he mumbled, pushing his glasses up the bridge of his nose.

"Whatever, Grandpa." This case had left me sore and exhausted. "All I know is that my junior secret agent days are over. Since the movie got suspended, I'm no longer on the case."

Grandpa looked disappointed. He folded his piece of paper.

"I'm not good at any of it, Grandpa."

He grumbled something, waved his hand like he dismissed my comments, and went back to his crossword puzzle.

I took a shower and got ready to go see Savannah sing and dance at the Hollywood Bowl. I agonized over what pants and shirt to wear, but in the end I settled on what I usually wore. Take it or leave it.

I grabbed my backpack, ready to head out the door. Dad's compass bounced against my side. I wondered if he'd ever get the car fixed. I should be helping him, like always. For the first time ever, I felt like I really didn't deserve to have his compass. I almost unclipped it but then changed my mind. Dad had given it to me when I went on my first mission, to Paris. *So you always know where home is.* Thinking of Melais selling that weapon to the terrorists on Monday made my chest hurt.

Before I left Grandpa, I said, "Oh, I forgot to tell you: Aunt Jenny wants you to come downstairs for food."

Grandpa made a face. "Store-bought beans and macaroni salad." No fooling him.

I shrugged. "Suit yourself." I opened the bedroom door, when Grandpa called me back.

"Lincoln, tell me something." He looked up from his crossword puzzle. "If your Flanigan guy—"

"His last name's Floyd, Grandpa."

"Floyd—if he already has your important artifact that's going to make him millions, then why did he cancel the movie?"

Grandpa had a point. Floyd could just hang tight, get the drone prototype, sell it to the terrorists, and be rich by lunchtime on Monday.

"I don't know," I said, tightening the straps on my backpack. "And I don't care anymore. Let the Pandora guys figure it out."

I left Grandpa with his crossword and hurried downstairs to snag Mike for a ride. I was going to see a beautiful girl perform. Who cared about a bad guy and puzzle pieces that didn't fit, right?

But as I hopped in the backseat of Mike's car, I had a nagging feeling in my gut. I didn't know it yet, but I should've listened to Grandpa.

Because the bad dude? He was waiting for me.

34

SATURDAY, 5:45 P.M.

MIKE DROPPED ME OFF AT THE PARKING lot on the west side, behind the actual Hollywood Bowl, after I listened to him and Willow go on and on (and on) about whether the muffler was making a funny noise. Mike thought so, but his girlfriend thought not.

I didn't care.

The air was cool, and I hurried across the packed parking lot to check in at the box office. There was a big banner for the Oscar weekend celebration tonight, with Ava Stone's name on it.

The lady behind the counter did a double take after she checked my name against the guest list. "You got a garden seat? You're lucky—but hurry up. The show's about to begin."

The lady wasn't kidding when she said I had a great spot. My seat had the best view of the Hollywood Bowl. The place is pretty much what you'd expect: a half-moon bowl over a stage, with seats that fan out into a valley-type setting. This was beyond awesome!

Onstage, Ava Stone was talking, so I was super quiet as I settled into my spot. "I'm so honored to be here tonight at the Hollywood Bowl. When people think of Los Angeles, they think of the movies. And that's why we're here: to celebrate the Academy Awards this weekend. But I'll always associate our great city with music—and all the great musicians who made silent film come to life." She smiled and continued, "Before there were talkies, musical composers were the heart of cinema—my grandfather was one of the greats."

You could hear a pin drop in the audience.

"It all started with great artists like Charlie Chaplin, of course—a genius who composed his own musical scores. Despite the fact that he couldn't read sheet music. Today we're here to celebrate his talent, and that of those artists who saw the good and the bad times, and continue to do so today. My daughter is here . . ."

I craned my neck to see Savannah just as my phone rang. I silenced it and almost didn't pick up, but then I saw the caller ID screen.

Unavailable. It might be important.

Someone in the audience gave me the stink eye for having a phone.

"Hello?" I whispered.

"Linc! It's Henry." It was almost impossible to hear him over the applause that erupted as Ava Stone left the stage.

"Dude, I can't be talking on the phone," I said, cupping my hand around my mouth so he could hear me. "Savannah is about to come onstage."

"That's why I'm calling!" Henry was practically screaming in my ear. "We're on our way over—me, Agent Stark, Ben, Albert Black."

"Why? You're not exactly invited, you know, and security—"

"Savannah has the Dangerous Double!"

I froze.

"Ethan Melais never had it. We finally got the security footage from Sterling Studios. It shows Kurt loading up the costume trailer on Thursday. Then Savannah meets him outside the warehouse, and he gives her a bundle of clothes."

"Her costume—she told me Kurt helped her," I said, slapping my forehead.

"He gave her a hat, too, dude. Kurt and Savannah probably had no idea it was a Dangerous Double."

Onstage, Savannah entered, doing some swirly dance. She was holding a bowler hat. That was the Dangerous Double!

It all made sense now. Savannah had been at Sterling Studios when I was there for the tour, and she'd told me about this performance, the authentic-looking costume she got from Kurt. I just hadn't put the pieces together.

"Oh no," I mumbled. I scanned the crowd for Floyd, but even if he was here, I wouldn't be able to spot him until it was too late. I could only hope he didn't know about Savannah having the hat.

"We're twenty minutes away," Henry said. I heard Albert Black grumble something in the background. "Okay, maybe more like thirty minutes, with traffic and stuff."

"That's not fast enough," I said, and hung up. Savannah's life could be on the line here.

Onstage, Savannah started singing. She was brilliant and beautiful. Her dancing was perfect, and if I hadn't been looking for Ethan Melais, I would actually have been able to enjoy her amazing performance. I scanned the crowd, behind me, around me. Behind Savannah.

This was impossible!

But then I thought I caught a glimpse of someone. A skinny blond guy, far behind me in the audience. He looked like Floyd!

Savannah was awesome. And I didn't want to ruin her performance—so what was I supposed to do? An annoying little voice at the back of my head told me that Ben would know what to do. But Ben wasn't here, so it was up to me to be the junior secret agent.

The blond guy had disappeared.

Was it Floyd? Where did he go?

I jumped up, ready to climb over people to chase my bad guy.

Then I heard a popping sound. And another.

Someone was shooting at Savannah.

35

SATURDAY, 6:15 P.M.

THE CROWD REALIZED WHAT WAS GOING on, too. There was screaming. People were shoving me as I ran to the stage.

Savannah did one more swirl and tossed the Chaplin hat into the air as part of her performance. But then she realized someone was shooting at her. She froze. The Dangerous Double bounced on the stage and rolled out of sight, away from the spotlight.

I used the stairs to the side, pushing a confused security guard out of the way to reach Savannah.

"Linc," she mumbled, looking dazed. "I'm so glad you came to see me perform."

"We have to go, Savannah," I said, grabbing her elbow.

We were sitting ducks there on the stage. I tried to spot the Double, but with the bright spotlights it was hard to see anything beyond my own feet.

More popping. I was pretty sure a bullet flew right over my head.

"Someone's shooting at you, Linc," Savannah said. She wouldn't move from her spot onstage. "That's funny." She smiled. This girl was in serious shock.

"No, it's not, Savannah."

Then I remembered: I had Henry's gadgets! I reached behind me and unzipped my backpack.

I opened the black box and strapped the watch gadget Henry had given me on my wrist. I pushed the tiny button twice. And activated the Three-by-Thirty. There was a slight green halo surrounding us.

"What's that?"

"It's a bulletproof shield," I said.

"It's so pretty." Savannah reached out to touch it.

"Don't do that," I said, slowly lowering her arm. I glanced around the stage one last time for the hat, but it was hopeless. I had to save Savannah first. "Just stay close, okay?"

"Okay." She smiled again.

I grabbed her hand. "You have to walk now. We only have thirty seconds." The watch told me I was already halfway out of time.

A bullet bounced off the halo. And another.

I pulled Savannah along and rushed off the stage. Another bullet skimmed off the shield. Whoever was shooting was still not done.

Could this case get any more deadly? And I wasn't even a real junior secret agent.

I hurried to get Savannah into the wings, where her mother whisked her away.

She was safe.

It wasn't until then that I realized something.

The shooting had stopped.

I turned around. Hurried to retrace our steps, back to where I'd last seen the Dangerous Double roll out of the spotlight.

I made it all the way back to the center of the stage, when I saw the black business card with the ivory letters that said *Ethan Melais*. And I realized it was too late.

The Dangerous Double was gone.

36

SATURDAY, 6:39 P.M.

THE LAPD SHOWED UP AND LOCKED DOWN the Hollywood Bowl so no one could leave until they left their name. The police were looking for the shooter, but I knew it was a waste of time. Ethan Melais had the hat, so he could disappear and walk right out.

I left Ben's name with the LAPD at the exit and made my way out of there, pretending to be just another visitor. And just as I walked toward the parking lot, he got out of a van and came running.

Ben Green. I saw Stark in the front seat, driving away to park the van in the crowded lot.

"A little late to the party, aren't you?" I said to Ben. I tried to brush past the guy, but then I realized that I still needed a ride. Behind me, the crowd slowly trickled out, as each person left their name with the police.

Ben glanced over my shoulder. "There was a shooting?"

I gave him the short version.

"You didn't secure the Dangerous Double first?" Ben frowned.

"I saved Savannah from Floyd." I felt like punching Ben, but deep down I was mad at myself for not having grabbed the Chaplin hat. It was right there onstage!

"It was right there onstage!" Ben yelled, like he was reading my thoughts.

I felt the edges of Melais's business card cut into the palm of my hand. I stuffed it in my pocket. "Maybe next time you can be here, huh? Where were you?"

"For your information, I was calling my contact at the CIA to see if there's a file on Nigel Floyd," he said with this righteous look on his face.

"And?"

"He's checking on it."

"How helpful."

Around us, people returned to their cars and left. I thought I saw that blue compact car, but when I craned my neck, traffic had made it impossible to see. I watched Stark park the van in the very back of the lot.

"What does your junior secret agent manual say we should do now?" I asked, half joking but sort of serious.

Ben sighed. "There are no procedures for this. The CIA didn't think we'd be retrieving Dangerous Doubles when they wrote the junior agent training manual. Pandora is black ops, remember? No manual, no record of their existence."

"Plausible deniability," I said.

"Exactly." Ben was quiet for a while and then asked, "Do you have any ideas?"

I had nothing. But I wasn't going to admit that. "I still don't get how Floyd knew Savannah had the hat."

"Maybe he already happened to be at the show and saw how old the hat was," Ben said. "It doesn't matter. We must locate Floyd and the Dangerous Double."

"Floyd has to be holed up somewhere with the Double, right?" I said.

"He'll go someplace safe. His home, or lair," Ben mused.

"Like his bat cave." As I said it, I knew where Floyd was. I could've told Ben. But since I'd just gotten shot at, I decided I should be the guy who caught the bad dude and brought in the Dangerous Double. Alone.

"You think he's at his house?" Ben asked.

"Could be," I said, and shrugged. "We'll pass it along to Stark and Black."

I could see Ben get antsy. His face got all serious—he had that secret agent look I hate so much.

I knew where Floyd was. Ben had a hunch, too. But neither of us was willing to share the glory.

At the far end of the parking lot, I could see a harried Stark, Black, and Henry walk our way, looking even more stressed than usual. LA traffic would do that to you. And now Pandora would want to be updated, no doubt.

"I'm going to check on Savannah," I lied, and walked back into the crowd.

Behind me, Ben called, "But you need to debrief!"

I turned around, smiled, and shook my head. "I'm not on the case anymore, remember?"

Ben slumped as he watched me walk away.

Not that I'd given up on catching Ethan Melais. Because I knew just where to find him.

37

SATURDAY, 7:05 P.M.

OF COURSE I WAS FACED WITH THE BIGgest problem any kid has when in Los Angeles: transportation. Since Savannah was recovering with her mother, I called my cousin.

Mike was only too happy to have another excuse to drive around. Naturally, that meant Willow was along for the ride, and I got to listen to them argue. This time it was about silent movies, and if they should remake them as talkies. Like I wasn't sick of that topic by now.

"All I'm saying is that it would be a better movie if people were talking," Mike said as he pulled in to Nigel Floyd's long driveway. "You could put in special effects." He grinned and nodded.

Willow rolled her eyes. "You just want to blow stuff up. That's *so* juvenile."

"Listen, guys," I said, leaning forward. "I'll get off here if you don't mind."

"You want me to stick around, man?" Mike asked. "I can come with you, too, whatever you want."

"Mike wants to be in the movies," Willow said in a teasing voice.

"Shut up." But Mike eyed me with a sense of hope. If he only knew that being cast in this movie meant you had a giant bull's-eye on your back.

I shook my head. "No, I'm just making this a quick visit." I would sneak in and get the hat. Then I'd call Stark and Black, have them catch Floyd. I would beat Ben. "I'll have a friend pick me up," I said as I opened the door.

Mike shrugged. "That's cool. You can always call me if you need something, okay, cuz?"

"Sure thing." I got out and watched Mike make a U-turn. I could hear them argue through the open windows.

I was glad to be alone, even if it was dark and quiet. Sure, this should be a slam-dunk, but I still had to get past Floyd's gates and security system. I kind of wished I had Henry with me now—he'd have a gadget for that.

Turns out I didn't need any help. The gate to Floyd's place was open, and the lights that had made the place look so fancy just two days ago were off. It made everything dark and deserted.

What was going on here?

I walked past the open gate, and up the winding driveway. No alarms went off, and no security guards stopped me. When I got to the circular driveway in front of the mansion, it was still dark, and the fountain wasn't running. This was seriously weird.

To get to the small house down the hill, I knew I had to go through the mansion. So I tried the front door. It was open. Now there were about a million alarm bells going off inside my head.

But I was after a bad dude here, so I couldn't just give up. I tried to be as quiet as possible when I went inside. I couldn't bump into tables or anything like that.

I didn't need to worry. The place was completely empty: no furniture, or art on the wall. Everything was gone, except for that fuzzy rug and the tables that hung from the ceiling. It was kind of sad, really. Obviously, Floyd had moved out.

My sneakers made squeaky noises on the marble floor, so I was careful to walk slowly as I found my way to the double doors and out to the deck. The lounge chairs were still there but were shoved to one side. I walked down the wooden steps and past the pool, where a half-deflated beach ball drifted in the water. This place was depressing.

Then I saw the house down the hill. The lights were on!

That had to mean my hunch was right: Floyd was here. Maybe leaving his mansion wide-open was just a ruse, to make us think he skipped town. He was probably plotting his heist of the drone-system prototype on Monday.

I walked down the steps, hoping Floyd wouldn't be using

the hat. I mean, it would be hard to catch him if he was invisible, right?

There was piano music coming from the house. It sounded like someone was actually playing. This was good. It would be hard for Floyd to hear me come in.

I tried the side door—it was open!

I snuck inside the mudroom. The piano music was much louder inside. Past the dark mudroom was an old kitchen. There was an open bread bag on the counter, along with a jar of peanut butter and chocolate spread. Dirty dishes were piled up in the sink, and clean ones were stacked on a dish rack. A few pots were left on the counter. This dude was kind of messy.

I slowly walked into the kitchen, and realized the music was coming from another room, at the end of a hallway at the back of the kitchen. I made my way toward the sound, down the hall, past some old pictures. They were of Floyd when he was much younger, and a few of Kate. I also saw photos of Larry, with dorkier glasses than he wore now.

Then the music stopped.

I froze. But I knew I couldn't wait there forever. I had to find Floyd!

I inched my way down the hall, careful to not knock down any pictures with my backpack. Once I reached the entry to what looked like the living room, I stopped. I saw the piano. But not Floyd.

I felt something brush against my arm. Maybe that was him, wearing the Dangerous Double!

I turned around, but there was no one there.

Then I felt someone grab my backpack. Pull me back. And tackle me to the floor.

Kate was right up in my face. "Linc?"

38

SATURDAY, 8:16 P.M.

SHE HELPED ME UP AND LAUGHED. "OH my, you scared the heck out of me. I thought you were breaking in."

"I was," I said, straightening my jacket and backpack. I really needed Henry to come up with a gadget so people couldn't tackle me by grabbing my backpack. An Escape-a-Pack or something. "But I was looking for Mr. Floyd."

Kate motioned for me to sit on the piano bench. "Why did you need him? The movie is all but finished, you know. I'm just here to get a few things I had stored here—I'm flying out of town for a new production late tomorrow night."

I tried to think of how to tell her about Ethan Melais without showing all my cards, or having to explain the whole case. But I couldn't think of a way. And Kate had been nice to me—in fact, she'd been the only friendly person on the set.

So I spilled my guts, again. About me being a junior secret agent, Pandora and their mission to catch Ethan Melais, and how Floyd was our only suspect left.

Kate sat on the arm of the sofa, nodding as I told her the story. When I was done, she shook her head, looking shocked. "I've known Nigel for years. . . . Unbelievable. And you really think he's this Ethan Melais?"

"Yes." I glanced around, hoping to find him hiding behind the piano or something. This house had to be his hiding spot—it was my best and only lead. If Ethan Melais wasn't here, then where?

"I'm sorry, but Nigel isn't here," Kate said, confirming my suspicions.

"Bummer," I mumbled.

"But then, if he is Ethan Melais, I'm sure he'll be back home any minute. With the movie being suspended now."

I was about to argue that Floyd already moved out—Kate had to know that, right? But then I saw how she crossed her arms, and looked . . . antsy. And a little nervous.

Kate was hiding Ethan Melais.

I knew it in my gut. So where was he?

Kate stood. "Well, I guess that's it. Nigel isn't here—you can look for him if you want," she added with a laugh.

I hesitated as I got up from the piano bench. My mind was racing, trying to think of an excuse, a reason for me to stick around longer and flush Floyd from whatever hiding spot he was in.

But Kate slowly ushered me down the hall, and I felt my opportunity slip the closer I got to the kitchen.

"Your Ethan Melais is quite the thief," Kate said behind me. "That takes some guts, to sneak into top-level meetings like that."

"Yeah." I glanced at the open bedroom door down the hall, but it was too dark to spot Floyd.

"What a character," Kate said once we were in the kitchen.

I turned around and looked her in the eye. Blinked. Because all the puzzle pieces fell into place now.

A character.

"Ethan Melais is a character," I said before I could think. "He's not a real guy. You're Ethan Melais!"

Kate smiled. "Finally, someone is smart enough to figure it out—an eleven-year-old."

"Actually, I'm twelve," I said.

Right before she grabbed the frying pan off the kitchen counter.

And hit me on the head.

39

SATURDAY, NO IDEA WHAT TIME

"LINC . . ." I HEARD SOMEONE CALLING my name through a tunnel. Or at least it sounded that way, because my ear was buzzing. "Linc!" There was a tap on my cheek. And another.

I opened my eyes to look right into Kate's.

She smiled and said, "Good, you're back."

Then I remembered: She was Ethan Melais. I had to bust her and find the Dangerous Double!

I tried to get up, only to realize I was cuffed to a kitchen chair. Ironically, Kate had used Henry's Instacuff.

"Stay awhile," Kate said. "At least until I figure out what to do with you." Considering this woman had tried to kill me three times already, I wasn't feeling so optimistic about my chances of survival this time around.

"I brought backup, you know," I lied. "CIA agents will be busting through that door any second now."

"No, they won't." Kate pulled up a chair and sat across from me.

We were in the middle of the kitchen. Behind her were the sink and the dish rack, full of plates and knives. All I had to do was get a knife and I could get out.

"So you've been Ethan Melais all this time," I said, ignoring the pounding headache I had from her hitting me with the frying pan.

Kate nodded, looking very proud of herself. "It started as a joke, if you can believe it. Nigel and I had just finished shooting a movie in Greece—he hated it, of course, just like all the films he makes. So over dinner one night, I jokingly suggested he put the movie out under a fake name. Directors do it all the time."

"Alan Something," I said, remembering my conversation with Savannah.

"Alan Smithee." Kate nodded. "But that was too obvious. Did you know 'Alan Smithee' is really an anagram for 'the Alias Men'?"

I closed my eyes, feeling like the biggest fool ever. Grandpa had figured this out long before—why hadn't I listened to him? "And Ethan Melais is, too."

Kate laughed. I would like to say it was an evil laugh, but she sounded like a regular, nice person. "The next day, I had some business cards printed, and I came up with a disguise.

As a joke." Her smile faded. "I was sitting in the hotel lobby, waiting for Nigel, who was late as usual, when I saw several men go into this meeting room. Since we had booked most of the hotel, I thought they were with the production company. So I decided to take my prank a little further, and I went inside the meeting."

I eyed the back door to the right of me, but no one was going to come and save me. And the cuffs were way too good. Thanks a lot, Henry. I had to keep Kate talking, to buy myself time to come up with a plan. "You stole a secret."

She nodded. "It was a sales meeting, unbelievably boring—but they were selling some high-tech computer chips. They thought I was a buyer, so I left the Ethan Melais business card. I sold the information to the company's competitors and used the money to help Nigel fund his next film. It kept me employed and him making movies."

"Everyone thought you were real—that Ethan Melais was a real guy."

Kate nodded. "To throw people off the trail, I started spreading rumors that Ethan Melais was French-Canadian, that he traveled the world and was a master of disguise." She smiled. "I had a blast creating this character. I figured it was only a matter of time before someone figured out he wasn't real, and made the connection to the 'Alan Smithee' or 'the Alias Men' anagram, but . . ."

"No one did."

"Until you, right now."

"Actually, my grandpa figured it out."

She leaned forward and got closer. Her eyes were hard—why hadn't I seen that before? "Those artifacts Pandora holds—I can't wait to get my hands on them."

"How did you know Savannah had the hat?" I asked, tugging at the Instacuff.

Kate smiled. "I did her makeup tonight and saw the costume. I was never going to kill her, you know."

"You were just accidentally shooting at her, right." I swallowed. "I could lie and pretend I won't tell anyone that you're Ethan Melais."

She let out a deep sigh. "But you wouldn't insult my intelligence."

"Now what are you going to do with me?" I might as well ask, since there was no way I could break free. Henry's Instacuff was too tight around my wrists.

Kate stood. "I never wanted you dead, Linc."

I rolled my eyes. "Oh, come on. You tried to kill me three times!"

"That's because I thought you had the Chaplin hat." Kate gave me a hard stare. "First I set off the runaway car—that didn't do the trick. You outsmarted me when I directed our chief cameraman, John, to put you in the current—or your brother, Ben, rather. Then you survived the Ferris wheel explosion . . ." She shook her head. "You're a tough kid to kill."

"I try." I pulled at the cuffs, but it was no use.

"And I shouldn't have bothered, because Savannah had the hat all along." Kate went down the hall, and came back with a bowler hat. That was the Dangerous Double! I was so close it was actually painful. Or maybe that was the bump from Kate hitting me on the head.

Kate smiled and turned on the gas stove. "I'm really sorry to have to do this to someone as smart as you. But I need to keep my identity a secret. I need for the authorities to be looking for Ethan Melais like he's a real person. And I need for them to think he's a man, not a woman."

I could already smell the gas.

"I'll light one of those dry bushes outside on fire, then all I need is for the gas to build up and . . . *boom.*" She lifted the hat, and carefully placed it on her head. "Wish me luck," she said, and tilted it.

Kate disappeared.

I watched the kitchen door open. And close again.

Leaving me there alone. Tied up.

To die.

SATURDAY, 9:05 P.M.

YOU KNOW DURING A TEST, WHEN IT'S so quiet you want to yell something random just to break the silence? It was even quieter than that in this kitchen. All I could hear were Kate's footsteps, then a car starting and driving away.

Then nothing. There was only the hissing noise of the stove, which wasn't exactly comforting.

I imagined one of the bushes on fire, right outside.

My mind was racing. I had to get out of this Instacuff! I needed magnets.

On the fridge! There were about half a dozen of them, up high. If I could get two of them, I could probably undo the cuff. I was stuck to the chair, but I could walk over. Sort of.

The stove was still hissing. And the place was beginning to smell like a bad fart. I had to hurry.

I reached the fridge and turned around so my back was against it. But the magnets were up too high to reach with my hands.

So I faced the fridge again. And inched one of the magnets down with my chin. But it fell to the floor.

I cursed under my breath. The gas kept hissing—and it was stressing me out big time. Plus the smell was making me sick to my stomach.

Magnet two inched down, and so did magnet number three—I turned to grab them with my hands. All I needed was to put them together and I'd be out of these cuffs.

But then I heard the footsteps on the path. Kate! She was coming back. Maybe she anticipated I'd be making a run for it.

With the magnets clutched in my palm, I backed away from the fridge, but then I realized I didn't care if she knew I was breaking free.

I was going to jump Kate when she walked in. With the chair still stuck to my back, I rushed to the door. Waited for it to open, ready to take down evil Kate.

The door opened.

And I bumped right into Savannah.

"Linc?" She looked over my shoulder. "What happened—who tied you up?"

"Kate did!" I pushed her out the door. "But we have to get out of here, now!"

Behind her, Ben was ready to go inside. "Baker? I should've known you'd start a fire."

"Out, now!" I yelled.

Thankfully, Ben and Savannah didn't question me—they followed me right up the hill, back toward the mansion. It's hard to hurry when you have a kitchen chair strapped to your back, let me tell you. When we reached the pool, Ben helped me undo the Instacuffs.

We both turned around to look at the house down the hill.

"I guess I could have turned off the stove," I said, more to myself than to Savannah and Ben.

"What?" I saw Ben mouth. But I couldn't hear him, because there was a giant explosion down the hill.

The house we'd left just minutes ago was now a ball of flames.

SATURDAY, 9:25 P.M.

WHILE WE WATCHED THE FIREFIGHTERS battle the blaze, Ben told me how Savannah came looking for me at the Hollywood Bowl. And how Ben had asked her for a ride to Floyd's house, because like me, he thought Floyd was Ethan Melais. Because Ben had had to debrief Stark and Black, he and Savannah were twenty minutes behind me. They'd gotten here just as the man himself got home with his assistant, Larry. But Floyd had an airtight alibi.

"I've been dealing with the repo men the rest of the afternoon and this evening," Floyd said. He sat down on one of the fancy pool chairs and kicked off his orange sneakers with a sigh. "It's all gone. The furniture, the house here, and the one downhill." Floyd pointed at the flames. "Well, that house is quite literally gone."

I asked Floyd, "So you didn't know Kate created a character, an international thief named Ethan Melais?"

Floyd gave me a confused look. "Does this have something to do with the car crash?"

I nodded.

"And the business with your brother almost drowning? Plus the Ferris wheel mess—Kate was causing all this?" Floyd looked shocked. There was no posing left in the guy, which was kind of nice. "I've been so distracted by the financial trouble. And before that, it was one film production after another. I only worried about the artistic side—the film, my vision. I was just happy when we got cash infusions when we needed them. Didn't ask where they came from."

I told them about Ethan Melais, the thefts, the money, and how Kate had used this character to go undetected for so long.

"Of course." Ben groaned. "We were looking for a man all this time."

"Kate." Larry sighed. "I thought something was off: the secrecy, the disappearances. I tried to find out more, but she was always one step ahead of me."

"Like a ghost," I said.

Larry nodded. "I followed her to your bedroom, Nigel. But then when I snuck inside, she wasn't there—just Linc here."

"That was you at the party, with the flashlight!" I said. At least I got that right.

Larry nodded. "But I couldn't report you for snooping without explaining why I was there."

"Who cares about all that?" Ben said. "Our suspect has just escaped! You blew the case," he said, pointing at me.

"How was I supposed to know Ethan Melais wasn't real, and that our bad dude is really a lady?" I wanted to get in his face, but my head hurt too much.

I called Mom and told her I would be on my way home soon. I lied and told her the performance was amazing. The family was so busy with the car overhaul and the reunion, I knew only Grandpa would be watching the news.

Ben got a phone call. Stark and Black had heard about the fire and were here. Savannah disappeared to tell her driver she was okay. While Ben briefed Albert Black, I met Stark inside the mansion.

"I'm glad you're okay, Linc," Stark said. "Although I wish you would listen when we say you're off the case."

"But Kate is on the loose with the Dangerous Double. Now what?" I asked, tightening the straps on my backpack.

Stark looked at me. "You've done an amazing job." Her voice echoed off the marble floors and the high ceilings. "Even though we only recruited you to be Ben's stand-in, you've done just fine as a junior secret agent."

Hearing Stark say this nice stuff about me made the whole almost-dying part not so bad. I only wished my parents were around to hear it. "You didn't answer my question."

"Honestly, Linc, there's no way to catch Ethan Melais—or Kate—in Los Angeles anymore."

I felt sick to my stomach. "So you're just going to let her steal that drone-system prototype and sell it to those evil terrorists?"

"We'll do our best in Las Vegas, since we know she'll be there." Stark touched my shoulder. "But until Monday morning's drone-weapon-prototype reveal, there's nothing we can do. Kate's invisible—she could be anywhere. We'll have to hope we can catch her there, using a Double Detector. But it's going to be tough."

I bit my lip so I wouldn't cry. I know I sound like a baby, but this was my family on the line.

"It's time for you to go back to your normal life." Stark stepped back. "You're off the case, Linc. For real this time."

42

SATURDAY, 10:30 P.M.

OF COURSE, GRANDPA DIDN'T LIKE THIS turn of events at all. After a cab got me back to my aunt and uncle's place, I checked in with Mom before heading upstairs.

Grandpa was waiting for me in our room, sitting in the wicker chair with his crossword puzzle. "No more mysteries to solve?" He slumped a little. "I was just getting warmed up over here."

"Sorry, Grandpa." I took off my backpack and sat down on the foldaway bed. "But this secret agent business should really be left to the professionals."

"Nonsense! You're as good an agent as any of those other guys." Grandpa wagged his finger at me. "You're better. You have heart, guts."

"Thanks, Grandpa." Truth was, I felt a little lost now that I was off the case. My family's lives were at stake. I felt like I should do something to catch Kate.

"So that's it?"

I pointed to the TV. "You and me, we're better off watching some crime shows." Well, at least Grandpa was.

I told him about the day, and how he'd figured out that "Ethan Melais" was an anagram of "the Alias Men" before anyone else.

"Tell me that part again," Grandpa said, so I did. The guy deserved the credit for cracking the case, even if I'd been too preoccupied to listen.

After I told the story for a third time, Grandpa got ready for bed, and I snuck down to the kitchen for some food. I'm pretty sure that almost dying makes you extra hungry.

The kitchen was at the back of the house, and from the window I could see the adults outside, talking, laughing, and having a good time. As I ate some crackers and cheese, I thought about Pandora. I would probably never see them again. And I didn't even get to say good-bye to my friend Henry.

Dad walked into the kitchen from the garage. "Hey, buddy." He looked tired as he sat down across from me and wrinkled his nose. "Did you sit too close to the campfire out there, Linc? You smell like smoke." Dad didn't realize I'd been gone.

"Sorry," I said. "Have you been in the garage all night?"

Dad rubbed his head. He groaned. "Rebuilding that Town

Car. It's like trying to get your grandpa to behave."

"Impossible." I slid my plate toward Dad to share, but he shook his head. "You need some help with the car?" I asked.

Dad looked at me and smiled. "That'd be nice. I missed you these past few days."

"Me too." My head was so full with the case, Pandora, and what was at stake. I could use a distraction.

I followed Dad to the garage. The Cadillac Town Car looked perfect on the outside: gleaming black paint, with shiny chrome, and dark-red panels on the sides. The engine was a different story. There were parts everywhere on the garage floor, but it wasn't as bad as I'd seen it before. "So what's first?"

Dad showed me the engine, the water pump, and the battery. It was a mess, but I'd helped him rebuild engines before. And it felt good to work together like always. By the time we were done and I looked up, it was almost two in the morning. "Whoa," I said.

Dad said, "We should probably wait until daylight to start her up."

"Yeah." I realized how quiet it was.

Dad smiled. "You know, let's break the rules for once." He opened the garage. "Start her up. Who cares if we wake everyone?"

When he tossed me the keys, I knew what to do. I got in and waited for Dad to stand over the engine, with the hood still up.

"Let's do it, Linc."

I turned the key in the ignition. There was a sputter, a bang. But then there was that familiar hum of the engine. "You did it!" I yelled to Dad.

He shushed me but smiled big. "We did it."

Of course, it took only thirty seconds for the whole Baker clan to crowd the garage in their pajamas. Uncle Tim high-fived Dad, and Aunt Jenny gave Dad their signature head rub.

It felt good to stand there in the garage with my family, watching the exhaust fumes blow away in the wind. But the Pandora case still nagged me, like a pizza-party stomachache.

"It's good to see you help your dad," Mom said, giving me a quick hug. "So no more movie business?"

"I'm done."

"You're not invited to the Academy Awards?"

I was about to remind Mom that it was the same time as the Baker barbecue, when I felt a sudden jolt of brilliance.

Kate! She was going to the Academy Awards—she had to.

"Linc?" Mom asked. "Are you okay?"

"Couldn't be better." I was going to catch Ethan Melais after all.

All I needed was a plan.

43

PLACE: MY AUNT AND UNCLE'S HOUSE

TIME: SUNDAY, 6:31 A.M.

STATUS: STUMPED, PRETTY MUCH.

THE ONLY PROBLEM? PLANNING IS NOT exactly my strong suit—I usually just roll with the punches. But this time, I would have to be the one throwing the first punch. And I had to be really, *really* smart to beat Kate.

No pressure or anything.

But now I could make it right. Get the Dangerous Double. Catch Ethan Melais, aka Katherine Freeman, and save my family—whether Pandora had kicked me off the case or not. And they had given up on catching Kate in LA anyway.

If only I could figure out how to do it. I'd spent most of the short night awake, thinking, while the coils of the foldaway mattress poked in my back. Except by six thirty the next morning, I heard Grandpa shuffle around the room, and I still had no plan.

I needed help. So I called my pal Henry and told him to meet me at the Perfect Frame Café at nine that morning. I had Mike drop me off.

Of course Henry had to show up with Ben and Savannah.

"I thought I told you to come *alone*," I whispered to Henry when he sat in the chair next to me.

"I needed a ride," Henry said. Then he smiled. "Plus, you said you needed brainpower, so the more the merrier, right?"

Ben looked most unmerry when he sat down across from me. Savannah just seemed uncomfortable.

"Are you okay?" I asked, since the night before hadn't exactly been easy for her.

"I'm fine, thanks to you. I feel kind of guilty now, leading Kate right to the hat. Henry told me about its special powers," she added in a whisper.

"You didn't know," I said. "And I'm just glad she didn't shoot you."

"Kurt told me he found the hat hidden behind some boxes on a top shelf in the costume warehouse. A lucky find, he called it." Savannah gave me a sad smile. "Not so much, huh?"

I said, "Let's just work on getting the Dangerous Double back, and catch Kate." I was kind of glad I had three friends here to help me now, even if Ben was part of our group.

Ben leaned on the table. "So what's your plan? If I'm going to break Pandora mission protocol, it had better be good."

I looked around to see if anyone was listening in. But the place was deserted, except for a dude at the counter. "Kate got nominated for an award, right?" I looked at Savannah.

She nodded. "Yes," she whispered, leaning on the table too. "For Best Makeup and Hairstyling."

"This year there are four nominees, so that makes her odds of winning one in four," Henry said. "That's a twenty-five percent chance. Of course, it also depends on politics and previous awards won, plus—"

"Let's stick with the one-in-four odds," I said, cutting Henry off. "Whatever her chances, she'll want to come, right?"

"The Oscar is the most prestigious award in the industry," Savannah said.

"But Kate can't really show her face," I said.

"There is a warrant out for her arrest." Ben nodded in confirmation. "The LAPD will be looking for Kate. The last thing she will want to do is show up at the Academy Awards today."

"See, that's where you're wrong," I said, knowing I was right about this. "Think about that profile we made of Ethan Melais, and everything we know about Kate. She wants—no, she *needs* the credit. Just like when she left the business card as Ethan Melais. She wants the recognition. Kate will show up for the Oscar. I feel it in my gut."

"Kate can just wear the Chaplin hat and go undetected," Savannah said.

"So let's catch her," I said. "The Academy Awards are our

one chance. Kate will have to wear the hat to make it inside."

"You're forgetting one thing." Savannah sat back in her chair. "Kate has to win, or she won't reveal herself."

"How about we con her?" I said, feeling that rush you get when you suddenly have a good idea. I looked at Henry. "Let's make the chances of Kate winning that Oscar one hundred percent."

Ben actually smiled. "If Kate wins, she'll have to come out of hiding to collect her award."

"And we steal the Dangerous Double." I smiled too. "Let's do it."

Now, this was more of an idea than a plan at this point. I had no clue how we were going to pull it off.

Savannah laughed and shook her head when we got to this part of the scheme. "You can't just rig the Oscars. There are strict security procedures on who handles the envelopes, and how they make it to the stage. On top of that, it's not like the jurors aren't aware of who they picked."

"But the con doesn't have to hold up for more than the moment it's announced," I said. "We just need Kate to believe she won, so she'll take off the hat."

"Couldn't you make a replica of the envelope?" Ben asked Henry. "Like you make your gadgets, only of the winning announcement."

Henry nodded. "I'll look at the footage of last year's award show to see what the envelope looks like. It can't be that hard."

"I know one of the people guarding the envelopes,"

Savannah said. "She works in the production office at *You Only Live Once*. I might be able to get away with a swap."

"Now all we need to do is get into the Chinese Theatre," I said.

"That's easy." Savannah smiled. "Mom can get me tickets; I'm sure of it. We're part of the acclaimed director Nigel Floyd's latest project, aren't we?"

"We are." I smiled. "People are dying to see us."

Ben nodded. "The Hollywood kids."

44

SUNDAY, 3:25 P.M.

THERE WAS ONLY ONE SMALL PROBLEM with our plan to take down Kate at the Academy Awards. And this time it wasn't a bad dude or lack of transportation holding me back.

It was the Baker family. I was supposed to be at the family barbecue that afternoon, and those reunion get-togethers went well into the evening. There was no way Mom would let me off the hook.

So as I stood at the bedroom window and watched my cousin Tara from San Diego struggle to find a parking spot out front, I tried to think of an excuse. Some fake story that would get me out of Pasadena and to the Chinese Theatre, where the Academy Awards were going down that evening with a special nod to classic movies. But I couldn't think of any lie that would sucker Mom and Dad into letting me go.

"What's wrong, Linc?" Grandpa looked up from his crossword puzzle.

"I think we have a chance to catch our bad lady."

"Really?" He closed the puzzle book, smiling. "I thought you were off the case."

"I'm trying to set things right." I sat down on the bed and told Grandpa about our plan to take Kate down at the Academy Awards. "It's risky. I mean, she tried to kill me four times: first the car, then the drowning, and the Ferris wheel. And at Floyd's house last night. I'm kind of scared."

Grandpa looked at me. He hesitated. "You know how I said I couldn't join the army because of my peepers?"

"Your eyesight was bad, sure." I hoped Grandpa wasn't going to tell that whole Geronimo story again. "Otherwise you would've been a parachute dude."

Grandpa shook his head. "My eyesight was fine back then. I went to the army recruiter's office, stood right outside for an hour. And then I chickened out."

I didn't know what to say to that. I mean, I told my share of fibs, but that was a big one.

"I let fear hold me back," Grandpa said. "These Pandora types keep calling you for a reason. I don't want you to not take the chance, be afraid, and—"

"Linc!" It was Mom, calling from downstairs. It was three thirty; I was supposed to meet Savannah at four to head to the awards. I was running out of time.

I sighed. "Coming!"

"Gimme a minute." Grandpa stood, and went downstairs.

I got up and slowly followed him. Maybe I could just sneak out, deal with the consequences later. This was a bad-lady takedown we were talking about. My family's lives were on the line. The stakes were too high for me to blow it off for a Baker barbecue.

But I didn't need to worry. Grandpa met me at the bottom of the stairs. With Mike.

"You're back on the job, Lincoln," Grandpa said. "No one messes with the Bakers, remember?"

"But what about Mom and Dad?" I asked.

"I've got you covered," Grandpa said. Then he leaned close. *"Agent Baker."*

I argued, "But I'm not an—"

"Shhhh." Grandpa handed a set of car keys to Mike. "He's driving you."

"In the new car? No way," Mike whispered.

Grandpa smiled. "Linc here is going in a Chaplin costume—gotta have the wheels to match."

"The family is letting me drive the mint 1940 Cadillac Town Car they just overhauled?" Mike's jaw dropped. "Man," he whispered.

"We're borrowing it," Grandpa said with a wink to me. "That's what family does: They take care of each other." Something told me no one knew about us borrowing the classic car Dad and I had worked on just last night. Mom always wonders why I get into trouble so much—I think

Grandpa's genes are to blame.

"Thanks, Grandpa."

Grandpa waved his hand like it was all nothing, but we both knew better. "I'm gonna get me a hot dog and some of that store-bought macaroni salad. You kids need to scram before anyone realizes I swiped the keys."

"Man," Mike whispered again.

Grandpa pushed us toward the door. "No fear. Go catch that bad lady, Linc."

45

SUNDAY, 4:45 P.M.

"THIS IS SKYLAR BROOKE, REPORTING live from the red carpet. I can sense the excitement in the air, can't you? Listen to those fans! Behind me, you can see Hollywood's hottest star, David Graham, with his new girlfriend, infomercial success Tiffany Pierce—don't they look smashing together?

"Oh, and here's Ava Stone with her husband, the musical composer John Stone. Aren't they the most graceful couple ever? And I hear their daughter, Savannah, will be making her own debut on the red carpet shortly. . . ."

We were watching the show on Henry's tablet, waiting just a few blocks away in the newly overhauled 1940 Cadillac Town Car. Mike was at the wheel.

"It worked," Savannah mumbled, smiling. She'd spent a few hours sending emails to reporters and making phone calls, to make sure the story buzzed in the media by the time the pre-Oscar entertainment started. Savannah had even gotten us tickets—her mother just made a few phone calls and it was a done deal.

"Savannah is going to arrive with the top secret junior cast of British director Nigel Floyd's much anticipated production, *The Hollywood Kid*. There have been some rumors that the production was halted, but representatives of the famous director have told us there are just some logistical delays. We're certainly going to get the scoop for you on that!"

"Man, this is so cool." Mike was following along from the driver's seat. He was wearing his prom tuxedo and was ready to drive us for our red-carpet arrival. Ben and I were both in Chaplin costumes and Savannah was in her 1930s dress—courtesy of Kurt the costume designer, who'd jumped into action when he heard we were going to the Academy Awards. Of course, he thought we were going there to promote the movie to get funding back. Lucky for us, word of Kate's criminal enterprise as Ethan Melais hadn't made it to the crew yet.

Henry was happy to stay behind. "I'll monitor the TV feed, in case stuff happens. You know."

"Perfect." I knew Henry didn't like to be out in the field. "We need you here," I told him.

Henry looked happy to hear that.

"When do we go?" Ben asked. He pushed the fake mustache down on his upper lip. "Aren't we going to be late?"

"We want to be the last to arrive," I said, reminding him of the plan. "That way Kate will already be inside, and we surprise the audience." I held up the Double Detector, the device we'd used to find the evil Mona Lisa on my first mission, in Paris. "I'll be able to spot Kate with this."

"It should work." Henry sounded nervous. "The Dangerous Doubles all have a heat signature of twenty-point-two degrees Celsius when exposed to light. At least that's my theory."

"It'll work," I said. I wasn't sure if I was just making Henry feel better, or myself too.

"Hey, cuz," Mike called from the front. "Watch the TV."

"Well, that just about wraps up our red-carpet preshow." Skylar hesitated, glancing at the street.

"We have to go," I said, and we all buckled into our seats. Mike drove the few blocks to the Chinese Theatre, where the Oscars were held, and Savannah told the security guards who we were. We pulled past a couple of roadblocks and past the paparazzi.

The place was packed. There were cameras all over the place, limousines pulling up or leaving, and lots of famous and not-so-famous people in fancy dresses and tuxedos. Suddenly I got really nervous.

I was at the Academy Awards!

"Awesome," Mike muttered in the driver's seat. He pulled up to a crowd of photographers on the red carpet. A lady wearing a silver dress and very high heels was talking into a microphone in front of a camera—Skylar Brooke.

I wiped my palms on my Chaplin costume pants and put on the bowler hat.

"And here they are!" I heard when I got out. I opened the back door so Savannah could exit the car. Ben was right behind her, and I realized that I looked like the limo driver or something.

TV show host Skylar Brooke interviewed Savannah, just like we'd planned. A bunch of paparazzi crowded us, pushing us out of the way to catch a picture of Savannah. So much for us being the famous Hollywood kids.

Ben and I slipped past the photographers and hurried down the red carpet. We passed all these celebrities posing for fans and photographers as we moved toward the entrance of the Chinese Theatre. I wish I could have stopped to take it all in, but we were on a mission.

"Let's get inside." I was about to push past the security guard, holding the Double Detector in my hands. But then one of the dudes grabbed me by the arm.

"No tablets or electronic devices allowed," he said in a burly voice.

46

SUNDAY, 5:05 P.M.

WITHOUT THE DOUBLE DETECTOR, WE had no way of knowing where Kate was.

This was not good.

The guard was muscular and looked like he was going to rip out of his black polo shirt if you ticked him off.

"I won't turn it on," I said. "Promise." I needed this gadget.

The guard shook his head—just once, but that's enough when you're buff like that. "Give it to me; I'll make sure you get it back when you leave."

I felt all my hopes sink as I handed over the Double Detector.

Ben was stressing out. "We're deviating from the mission

plan," he whispered once we were inside.

"Stuff happens," I said. "We'll find her some other way." But I felt worried, too. Without the Double Detector, I couldn't spot Kate. She could be anywhere.

A couple of butler-looking guys ushered us to the entrance of the actual theater. A lady in a black dress checked her guest list and then pointed to the very, *very* back of the theater.

"This is good," Ben said as we were put in our back-row seats, the only spots left at such short notice. We both took off our hats and held them in our laps. "We can observe the whole theater," Ben said, and started with his mission right away, scanning the crowd.

Like we'd actually be able to see Kate. Although I knew she was here, right now. I could feel it. Or maybe it was Ben's tension messing with my senses.

"Dude, you need to relax," I said. I leaned away, trying to distance myself. "Let the plan work."

"But what if it doesn't?" Ben gave me a stressed-out look. "We already lost the Double Detector. What if Kate doesn't show up?"

"She'll be here," I said, sounding more confident than I felt. "And Savannah is in place as we speak, ready to swap the envelopes."

"But what if—"

"Just trust me," I hissed. Thankfully, the theater lights dimmed. I couldn't wait to lose my annoying look-alike.

Ben asked, "How long before they announce the award?"

* * *

One time, Mom roped me and Dad into going to see this really long movie—an epic saga, it said in the commercial. Epically boring was more like it—only this Oscar ceremony was about a thousand times more snoozeworthy than that. First there was the screen test; then there were the awards for Best Grip or something.

"If Kate is around," I muttered, "maybe she'll fall asleep and lose the hat."

"This is excruciatingly dull." Even Ben agreed.

Of course, it was pretty cool to be there in this old theater filled with movie stars. If I hadn't been there to catch a bad lady to keep my family alive, I probably would've enjoyed it more.

Onstage, a guy in a suit droned on about the importance of makeup artists to the movie industry. "And the nominees are . . ." Everyone looked up at the TV screens on both sides of the stage.

"That's our cue," I whispered as I put my Chaplin hat on my head. Ben and I got up.

We had one shot at this. When Kate walked up to the stage, she'd have to lose the Dangerous Double's invisibility powers. It was our only chance to steal the hat. Ben and I rushed to the front, then inched closer to the stage steps, him on the right, and me on the left. If Kate was here, she'd be coming this way.

"And the winner is . . ." The dude in the suit opened up the envelope.

For a split second, I worried that maybe Savannah's

switching of the envelopes had been foiled. But I didn't need to worry.

The guy opened up the envelope and smiled, quickly hiding his surprise. "Katherine Freeman!"

Music got loud, and the cameras swooped in. Ben and I exchanged a glance and then started to look for Kate. Trouble was, she was like a ninja—only worse. She could come from anywhere in the audience.

The audience started looking around too, and so did the dude in the suit. What if Kate didn't show up? What if our character profile was wrong and she didn't care about the Oscar? What if she was already on her way to Las Vegas?

"There she is!" the guy on stage exclaimed with a relieved laugh. But Ben, Savannah, and I were far from relieved.

Because Kate was already walking up to the microphone.

She'd been hiding backstage all along.

SUNDAY, 6:25 P.M.

THIS WAS REALLY, REALLY BAD. OUR best chance to get the Dangerous Double was when Kate walked from the audience up onto the stage. And now she was already there!

Ben and I looked at each other, but there was nothing we could do but listen to Kate thank the studio. She wore a tuxedo, only it was made for a woman. Probably to make the Chaplin hat appear like it was part of the look.

She spoke softly, "There have been a lot of obstacles in my way over the course of my career. This award means a lot to me. Getting recognition from my peers is priceless." Kate held the award in her left hand and the Chaplin hat in her right. She looked up at the audience on the balcony of the theater, and was silent for what seemed like forever. Her eyes were wet. "Thank you."

Kate moved to walk behind the stage, where she'd come from.

"Now what?" Ben mouthed.

There was only one thing to do. We had to follow Kate backstage!

Apparently Ben had the same idea, because he rushed after her, clutching his Chaplin hat. Savannah was waiting in the wings. Music sounded overhead, and some voice-over talked about Kate winning her first Oscar.

Ben and I made it backstage before any of the security dudes could stop us. Kate was walking down some steps. We couldn't let her get away!

Ben elbowed me, like I needed a hint. I knew this was our last chance!

But Savannah was way ahead of us. She hurried after Kate, then tapped the bottom of the Dangerous Double out from under Kate's arm.

Sending it flying high in the air.

Savannah jumped to catch it, so she now held two bowler hats.

Kate spun around to snatch it back, but Savannah did one of her pirouettes to get out of Kate's reach. Around us, backstage TV crew looked surprised, but then smiled. They thought this was a joke. The security guards that had followed us backstage looked confused.

Savannah tossed a hat to Ben. Ben tossed one to me. I

passed one back to Savannah.

"Give me my hat back, or I'll—" Kate realized she was surrounded by a bunch of bystanders, and shut up.

But I didn't. "It's kind of hard, isn't it, now that you're not wielding a frying pan!" I tossed a hat back to Ben.

"Give me my hat!" Kate screamed, not caring who heard.

Ben passed a Chaplin bowler to Savannah. Beforehand, at Kurt's costume trailer, we'd distressed the costume hats so it would be impossible to tell which was the Dangerous Double. Just in case we needed to make a quick swap.

Kate looked furious as her eyes darted between the three of us. "It's mine! I deserve this recognition!" she hollered, waving her Oscar statue, "and that!" She charged toward Savannah.

Ben and I both jumped to cover Savannah, right before the double doors opened with a bang behind us.

"LAPD! Nobody move!"

48

SUNDAY, 7:05 P.M.

AND JUST LIKE THAT, THE PLACE WAS crawling with dudes and ladies with guns, looking super gung ho to take down Katherine Freeman, aka Ethan Melais. Ben, Savannah, and I made sure we stayed out of the way. The TV crew stepped back, after one of them pried the Oscar statue from Kate's fingers.

I tossed my costume hat aside and clutched the Dangerous Double. Kate may have thought Savannah had it, but it had wound up in my hands. No way I would let go of it now.

Agent Stark zoomed by me and managed to cuff Kate before the police officers took over. I swear, I saw a smile on Stark's face as she secured the handcuffs—a real smile. She'd gotten her bad lady and set things right. "Not so tough without your makeup and disguise, are you, Ethan Melais?" Stark said to Kate.

Kate just gave her a nasty look, before Stark handed Kate over to one of the police officers.

"How did you know to come here?" I asked Stark.

Stark said, "Black and I were nearby, hoping Kate would show up. We figured it might be a last opportunity to catch her. Then we saw her accept her award on TV—and so did the LAPD. Is that the Dangerous Double?" she asked, pointing at the Chaplin hat I had clutched against my chest.

"Yes. But I want to get it to Albert Black." I'd completed the mission. And I wanted to get the credit for completing the mission, even if my family would never know I'd saved their lives.

Stark understood. She nodded, and glanced around. "We need to leave before our law-enforcement friends start asking too many questions."

Stark flashed her badge and whisked Ben, Savannah, and me out through the double doors.

Once we got to the lobby, Savannah grabbed my hand. "I have to get back to my mom and dad," she said softly.

I glanced over my shoulder, with the Dangerous Double tucked firmly under my arm. Agent Stark and Ben were waiting near the exit. "I have to finish this mission."

She smiled. "This was fun. Scary, but cool, too."

"I know."

Savannah let go of my hand and pulled a white business

card from her pocket. "You can have your people call my people."

I laughed.

Savannah put the card in my palm and folded my fingers around it. Then she left to go back inside.

Stark escorted us out. "Black is parked up the street," she said as we passed more police officers. They were busy creating a perimeter, holding back the paparazzi, camera crew, and fans.

The three of us hurried down Hollywood Boulevard. I felt kind of conspicuous in our period costumes. Ben and I both wore our bowler hats, the ones with *Made in China* embroidered on the label inside the rim.

I held the Dangerous Double tight. I couldn't wait to leave it with Black, let me tell you. Stark ran ten feet ahead, with Ben on her tail. Once we reached the van, Henry opened the door on the passenger side.

I sat down on the bench, catching my breath.

Henry asked, "Is that the Double?" He pointed at the bowler hat in my lap.

I nodded.

Albert Black held out a hatbox, and I put it inside. It was like a giant weight lifted off my shoulders.

"Nice work, you two," Black said, turning in the driver's seat. "Another Dangerous Double secured for Pandora. We confiscated film footage of *The Hollywood Kid*, so Agent Green's cover remains intact. The defense summit is secure now that Ethan Melais and the Dangerous Double are no longer a threat. Our job here is done."

I cleared my throat. "Well, I guess I should go," I said. "My cousin is waiting a block away." I didn't want to leave. Sure, these missions were deadly, and I was happy we'd secured this Dangerous Double. But I would miss being a temporary junior secret agent with Pandora. It was the only time my troublemaking talents were appreciated.

I knew it was time to go.

"Thanks, Linc," Black said. Ben gave me a wave, and Henry did a fist bump. Stark gave me her signature nod while she opened the van's sliding door.

I got out and walked away, toward the alley where I'd told my cousin we would meet. Behind me, I heard Albert Black rev the engine and drive away. I forced myself not to turn around, because that would be wimpy, right?

I knew this was it. My Pandora days were over.

EPILOGUE

PLACE: MY HOUSE

TIME: SOMETIME IN MAY

STATUS: BACK TO BEING A REGULAR KID

AFTER THAT, IT WAS BACK TO NORMAL for me. Back to early-morning skateboard rides to school, getting in just before the bell. Sometimes, when I saw a black sedan, my heart would freeze. But after a few weeks, I knew: Pandora was never coming back for me. I'd had three cool missions. Time to leave the junior secret agent craziness to Ben. I told myself it was better that way.

A few weeks after my mission in LA, I heard that Ava Stone was funding Nigel Floyd's *The Hollywood Kid*. Shooting would start fresh, with Savannah cast as the only kid—pretty cool, I thought. Savannah got an Xbox for her birthday, and would message me sometimes.

Months passed, and I stopped looking for dark sedans. Then on Friday, a few weeks before summer break, Mom knocked on my bedroom door. I was just about to level up on my new game, Racing Mania Ten, so I may have sounded a little snappy. "Yeah?"

Mom turned off the gaming console. Not cool.

But I bit my tongue just in time. "Sorry, Mom. What's up?"

"There's someone here to see you. An adult, Linc." She smiled, then left my room.

Uh-oh. As I put the controller away, I tried to think of what trouble I'd been into lately—let's face it, I was good at that. But aside from an incident involving the teacher's pens and superglue, I couldn't think of anything that would warrant an adult coming to see me.

So when I walked into the living room, I felt kind of nervous. And then I saw her.

"Linc," Mom said. "This is Anna Waters."

It was the lady with the gray pixie cut, the one I'd seen on my first day in LA! She smiled and shook my hand. "Nice to meet you, Linc. Of course, I feel like I already know you."

Dad spoke up from his spot on the couch. "Ms. Waters has been following your progress, ever since that class trip you took to Washington, DC."

Grandpa sat in his ratty recliner, doing his crossword, but I could tell he was listening in.

"You were checking up on me," I said to Ms. Waters,

before I could think. And I knew by the way she moved, by the black lace-up shoes she wore: Ms. Waters was actually *Agent* Waters.

Everyone sat down in the living room.

Agent Waters smiled. "We do a background check on all our prospective students. You've changed quite a bit during the past six months."

I'd been diving from an airplane in Paris, defusing a bomb in the White House, and hanging off a Ferris wheel after bad dudes tried to kill me. That was bound to change a kid at least a little.

"We think so," Mom said. She held a brochure.

"What's that?" I asked.

Agent Waters said, "I'm a representative from an elite training academy."

"Ms. Waters is offering you a full scholarship, Linc." Mom looked nervous. She handed me the brochure.

Dad said, "It's up to you, buddy. I'd sure love your help around the shop, but . . . this is an incredible opportunity."

Agent Waters added, "You can come back again during school vacations, and each summer—if you want."

I looked at the brochure. There was a fancy-looking building on the front, and the usual boring description inside, to impress the parents. But then I read the fine print at the very bottom. *Pandora, Inc.* Truth was, I felt kind of nervous. And a little scared—what missions and bad dudes were waiting for me if I said yes?

Grandpa looked up from his crossword. He didn't need

to say anything—when you're family, sometimes you already know what someone's going to say before they do.

Geronimo.

Grandpa smiled.

And that's how I ended up joining Pandora as a junior secret agent—for real this time. So if you hear some news report about strange things happening in Rome or London, or even in some small town in the middle of nowhere, it might just be about a Dangerous Double and Pandora.

And about me. Agent Linc Baker.

You believe me, right?

ACKNOWLEDGMENTS

My name is on the cover, but it takes a team to turn Linc's story into a book. Here are my humble thank-yous.

First, thanks to my agent, Stephen Barbara, for always knowing just what to say, and adding priceless creative input. He's kind of a rock star, I think.

I may be far away from New York, but a phone call with HarperCollins Children's always makes me feel like I'm right there. Many, many thanks to my editor, Alexandra Cooper, who is brilliant, meticulous, and kind—she's every writer's dream editor. Thank you to Alyssa Miele, for helping make the story so much better. Thanks to all the people at HarperCollins Children's who make this book look (and read) fantastic.

A writer needs friends, and I have them all over the globe. Thank you to Deb and Jenny, my friends in Colorado, Wordsmiths, and SCBWI Southern Breeze for making me feel at home.

My family in Holland gets extra credit this time, for giving me inspiration for Linc's wonderful family (minus the cars and grumpy Grandpa anyway). Thank you to my parents for fostering my love for books and libraries.

Thank you to Jason for allowing me to disappear into an imaginary world when I needed to. To my daughters, Tyne and Nika, who have the best imaginations (thanks for the great ideas!).

Last but not least: thank you to my devoted Linc fans. You make all the difference.